The Streets Are Calling

Lock Down Publications and Ca$h Presents

The Street Are Calling
A Novel by *Duquie Wilson*

Lock Down Publications
P.O. Box 870494
Mesquite, Tx 75187

Visit our website @
www.lockdownpublications.com

Lock Down Publications
Like our page on Facebook: Lock Down Publications @
www.facebook.com/lockdownpublications.ldp
Cover design and layout by: **Dynasty Cover Me**
Book interior design by: **Shawn Walker**
Edited by: **Tisha Andrews**

Stay Connected with Us!

Text **LOCKDOWN** to 22828 to stay up-to-date with new releases, sneak peaks, contests and more…
Thank you.

Submission Guideline.

Submit the first three chapters of your completed manuscript to ldpsubmissions@gmail.com, subject line: Your book's title. The manuscript must be in a .doc file and sent as an attachment. Document should be in Times New Roman, double spaced and in size 12 font. Also, provide your synopsis and full contact information. If sending multiple submissions, they must each be in a separate email.

Have a story but no way to send it electronically? You can still submit to LDP/Ca$h Presents. Send in the first three chapters, written or typed, of your completed manuscript to:

LDP: Submissions Dept
Po Box 870494
Mesquite, Tx 75187

DO NOT send original manuscript. Must be a duplicate.

Provide your synopsis and a cover letter containing your full contact information.

Thanks for considering LDP and Ca$h Presents.

Acknowledgments

I want to give all praise to, Allah, the high and merciful, may peace and blessings be upon him. And to all of my brothers and sisters of Islam.

To my mother, Jackie, who has always been in my corner even when I wasn't in my own corner, I love you dearly, thank you for giving me life.

To Kerry Saint Juste; my heart, my baby, I thank you for you being you, if I can't count on anybody else I know that I can count on you, Mama, you've showed me a love so unblemished and for that I will forever love your entire being, I love you.

To my two Godmothers; Teniel, Michelle, and Samone, I love you all, thank you for loving me unconditionally.

A heartfelt R.I.P. to the following people; Joyce, Arnold, Linwood, Khalilah, Brenda, Jean, Ronette, Rafee, Keyon (Kanye), Raymond Faison Sr., Sadie Maye Brown, Tay Tay, Dale, Rock (Malika's brother), Tashawn Qualls, Ruffin (Flip) Qualls, T-Man, Dena, Aunt Leola, Uncle Charles, Jeffery, J.D., Yameel, Fuzzy, Capo, Ernest (Ern) Bradley, Su, Ruger Rell, Weez, Bleep, Ruger Rell, Justin Bailey, Thomas (T. Turn) Turner, Millz, Hass a.k.a. Bishop a.k.a. Hard Body, Na, Lil Mikey, Fatal, Eric (Uggie) Bowens, and all my other loved ones that are not here to witness this, keep watching over me.

To my aunts; Barbara, Michelle, Rasherra, Judy, Mattie, Jacinta, Ellen, Badia, Chrystal, Julie and Niecy Rutledge, and Joyce, thank you all for being there to care for me at different points within my life.

To my Uncles; Gary, Steven, Tony, Stanley, Gilbert, Yah Yah, Michael (Ya Heard), Musafa, Fateem, and Michael Wright, much love goes out to y'all.

To all of my sisters and brothers; Tahannah, Quetta, and Quadir Prince, Donte and Khashana Williams, Jazmin, Jamar Cotton, Samir, Gregory (L.I.) Baker; the love you've shown me over the years is surreal, Vernon Williams, and Chrystal Colbert I love y'all.

To my cousins; Sheila, Khalilah, Karen, Qiana, Spring, Abaya, Vito, Keisha, Kumar, ShaQuan, Shakeir, Natasha, Mark Clark, Marcus, Nakita, Myu, Fee, Memph Man, Nay Nay, RaQuan, Terry, Sha Sha, Cam, Flame Thrower, CK, Big Head, Adris and Andre Scott, Brittany and Russell Jenkins, Derrick, Darren, Aja, Quan, Kevin, Javon, Jakaii, Demetrius, L, Ibn (730) Gordon, Sharese, Lonzel, Na Blood, Brazy Boy, Bang Ru, Trisha, Ida, Sharod, Cookie, Dada, both Pookie's, Iiesha, Curtis (Scootie) and Connie Williams, Karrelle, Nucci Reyo, Jason Johnson and his brothers, and to the rest of my cousins that I didn't name, you know who you are, I love each and every one of y'all. Shout out to Mira, I can't forget you.

Shout out to my lil homies; Rodney Williams aka Killa and Michael Marcano aka Loco both from Jersey City, and Eskay from Rahway.

Shout out to Pistol Pete, free a real nigga already!!! Shout to Peter Gunz, and the whole Soundview Projects in the Bronx, New York.

Shout out to my High and Spruce, Astor Street, and Muhammad Ali Avenue family; Fat Cat a.k.a. Skoob, Dave Blood, Lexx, Shaqir (Wink) Scott, Dell, Coop, Who Blood, D-Block, Duke, Blillz, B.I.P. Bimby, Rell aka Beez, D-Trick aka B.H., One Pac, J-Hood, Wally Mu, Slug Illz, Gunn Illz, Choppa, my cousin Pike aka S.P. and his brother

Al-Q, Ladybug, Vanessa, Hard 2 Kill, Deen a.k.a. Buz, Stretch, B-Shiest, Spudd, Kay, Rah Jigga, Monkey, Yoge, Mall Wally, Malika; As salaamu alaikum Ms. Claiborne, Mudda, Melissa, Taj a.k.a. Boy Blood, Carwash, Qiana, Twin, Samone, Kiya, Anna, Meeka, Rusty, and everybody else that I couldn't mention.

I gotta shout my nigga; Dopeboy from Da Land, Do-Low from the South Ward, Wadood (Soody) Peterson, Mack Black, Born from Rahway, my nigga Hard Hat, Baby from 18th and 18th, Carlos (C-Lo) Cosme, my nigga Jerome (J. Jay) Hudson, Anthony (A.C.) Carlesimo, Lameer (Meer) Graves, Kyle (Kash) Champagne, Benjamin (B.H.) Henderson, Ebony Collins, Kwik Ru, Shawn and Harold Cook, I tip my hat to the homie Tutt; the streets missing you, skoob, to Ransom; pain is truly glory my nigga, Montega Bino, Sharuffin (Pumpkin) Qualls, Robert (Champ) Bowman, Brenston (Silk) Ayers, Anthony (CK) McGriff, Floyd Wilson from Jersey City, Eric (Squeeze) Smith, Tony Martin, Corey (Y.G.) McIntosh, D-Money from Jersey City, Broderick Melvin, Michael (Rico) Del Valle from East Trenton, Lumidee, Twin from Plainfield, Ant Fountain, Quabisha (BeBe), June, Fritz, Nyiesha, Man, Risha, Neek, Auntie, Christina, Radika, Jungle, Ruck, Jameek, Kenny, Meeka, Lil Man, CeCe, Brock, Louie 13th, Larry Lincoln, Daryl Martin, J Bone, Jerome (Roc), Joey (Buddens), Jeremy, Roy and Shelly Gilbert, Brittany M., Monique, Draper, Noyd, Shameek, Sha Kim, Double S, Naeem, Slink, Moch, Bam, Pill Head, T-Relli, Born Brim, Shawn Campbell, Nane, Heff, DJ Kayslay, Folashade Adewale, Chyna Bricks, G.G. (Golden Girl), Jalissa (Kream) Moody, Lady a.k.a. Charlie, Deek, Mya, Sameerah Henderson-Turner, Nya Shell, Sheed, Darren (D-Block) Brown, Lakiesha Cook, Phillip (Banks) Turner from Millville, Samantha Brooks; who allowed me the time to write while I was in the halfway house, Hussain (Crush) Wright, Redman, Kerwin Delva; thank you for the ear when I needed it the most, and all of those that I missed, just know you wasn't forgotten.

I want to send a lustful shout out to a few beautiful women such as; Becca Banks, Stacie Lane, Nia Long, Remy ma, Chayna Ashley, Michelle Rodriguez, Shay Johnson, Eve, Tiffany Withers, Asa Akira, Dej Loaf, Ryan Destiny, Cherokee D'Ass, Keyshia Cole, Megan Good, Lola (Angel) Love, Janelle Monae, Kat (Ms. Kat) Washington, Treasure P., Jhonni Blaze, Simone Giles, Cardi B., BeBe Chi-Town, Ms. Hustle, Lil Nat, and Kimberly Elise.

My literary inspirations are Al-Saadiq Banks, J.M. Benjamin, Wahida Clark, Ca$h, Donald Goines, Michael Myers, Supreme Understanding, Nisa Santiago, James Patterson, and Brick City Riq.

And to my readers, I thank you most of all, I write with the vision that you see the picture as I see it and understand the movement behind every page that you turn

Duquie Wilson

PROLOGUE
Sunday
September 15, 2013
Irvington, New Jersey

"Aaaggghhh! Please, I swear it wasn't—"

"Shut the fuck up! When Soo's money comes up short, then my mu'fuck'n money comes up short! And I don't have sympathy for the nigga that caused that!" Pont barked, standing over the man tied to the chair drenched in blood.

"I swear to God, Pont! It wasn't me, man!"

"Who was left in charge of your block? You! Who hands did I put the drugs in? Yours! So who do I blame? You!" he snapped, swinging the hammer with deadly force, crashing into the man's collarbone.

"Aaaggghhhhhh!"

"Pain is the answer for your fuck up, but death will compensate for the loss that I just took."

Pont stood in the center of an abandoned basement with a construction worker's tool belt wrapped around his waist. He was delivering pain to one of the soldiers he'd hand picked to run one of his blocks. Behind him were three beefed up bodyguards staring on as he inflicted sheer pain on the young hustler.

Behind them was the head nigga in charge, Soo, sitting in a black lawn chair. He was smoking a $1,200 Gurkha Black Dragon cigar, overseeing the work of his top soldier. The room was dim but lit by the streetlights outside, crashing against each wall, lighting the room just enough to leave the wondrous rats in fear.

The room smelled of cigar smoke, old piss, mold, dog shit, and stale living. However, Pont was used to the stench because of repeated trips down there. The young hustler was tied down to a wooden chair by rusted chains. His top two soldiers were beside him, their clothes stripped from their bodies except their boxers. The other two kids had their mouths duct taped shut, their eyes wandering around the room for any sign of hope.

Pont gave the young hustler one more reassuring smile before drawing his chrome P-89 ruger, aiming it at the kid's head as he wrapped his finger around the trigger.

"Please, Soo. I'm begging you not to do this," the kid pleaded, piss flowing down his leg from excruciating fear. "I can make this right! I swear on my life!"

"Now you see that's where we have a problem because your life means nothing to me anymore," he countered, his face straightening back up.

"Please!"

"Shut the fuck up!"

Blok! Block! Block! Block! Block!

The kid's body jerked forcefully as each bullet entered his body effortlessly, blood splattering in several different directions that painted Pont's grey True Religion t-shirt, the walls, and the floor. You could hear the pounding of the other two soldiers' heart as they witnessed their close friend murdered. A fate they dreaded to meet.

Pont walked toward the kid to his left and raised the gun carelessly. The young boy began to tussle violently, trying to fight for his freedom. Pont put a bullet in his head without a blink of the eye, the boy's head snapping back as his blood created a pattern against the wall behind him. Next, he walked over to the third hustler and pressed the smoking hot barrel against his forehead, causing the kid to squirm from the pain.

"You're gonna make sure that this never happens again. You go back out there and regroup. You find out who caused my money to come up short, and trust if this happens again, I'm gonna kill you and your entire family," Pont declared, staring the kid square in his eyes. "Make sure you never forget this night."

The kid nodded his head as Pont turned around and looked at Soo. Soo nodded his head and said, "Clean this up and get back to work. I gotta go outta town for a while. When I get back, I expect things to be back to business as usual."

"I got this," he said, watching Soo stand up with the calm of no return. "Y'all heard what he said. Get this shit cleaned up and make sure this mu'fucka gets back to the block in one piece."

Duquie Wilson

CHAPTER 1
Tuesday
September 17, 2013
12: 45 p.m. Newark, New Jersey

"Allahu akbar," Tah said, declaring that Allah is great in Arabic. He raised his hands up to his ears and bent over, leveling his head with his back as he came into ruku. Tah placed his hands on his knees, making sure to spread his fingers. His eyes focused on his prostration. "Subhana Rabbiyal Aadheem," he said, meaning glory to my lord, the almighty.

Tahiem "Tah" Muhammad was a faithful and firm believer of Islam. So, no matter what he was doing, he would stop to offer salat which is prayer. He had been Muslim since the very day he was born. He didn't, however, really take to his deen until he was maybe around six-years old.

Within those trying years, he had a bag full of blessings that changed his outlook on life. He would never again challenge nor question the mercy of Allah also known as God. Tah stood there in his closet dressed in a dark grey t-shirt that hung down to his shins which was his Islamic garbs. Underneath, was a pair of black Sean John linen pants. He used his closet for salat because there were no windows or pictures there. Just his Qur'an and his musalla also known as prayer rug.

"Sami' Allahu Liman Hamidah," Tah said, raising back up to a standing position. That means Allah listens to who whom praises him. "Rabbana Wa Lakal Hamd Allahu akbar," he finished, which meant our Lord, praise is for you only.

Sitting in Tah's bedroom on his full size bed was Tahiry Giselle, Tah's best friend and side chick since he was four-years old. Many people thought Tahiry was Tah's girlfriend, but she was the one he always ran back to. She stood five feet tall with the facial essence of the beautiful model, Melyssa Ford.

Their relationship was open, understanding that boundaries should never be crossed. She still dealt with other dudes while he dealt with whomever he dealt with. Their history made them good together. They knew when to turn it on and when to turn it off.

Tahiry didn't really have a religion so to speak, but she did believe that there was a God. However, she had the utmost respect for Islam, thanks to Tah, Phenom, and Champ.

"Daddy, paying?" thirteen-month old Malani asked, trying to pronounce the word praying as she showed her innocence, sitting on Tahiry's lap as she ate a pear.

"Yup, your daddy is in there praying for all of us," Tahiry replied, looking deeply into the beautiful chocolate eyes of her niece.

"Llah bar!" Malani cheered, trying to say Allahu Akbar.

"Good girl," Tahiry said and smiled, hugging Malani tightly against her chest. She then lovingly kissed her on top of her head.

Tahiry sat there in a silver Sean John velour suit with a pair of black on black low top Nike Air Force Ones. Malani sat on her lap with her red Juicy Couture sundress with her Pampers pull-up sticking out of the bottom. Tahiry loved Malani as if she'd spent ten months in her womb instead of Sandy's, her mother. She respected Tah highly for stepping up to the plate and being a great father at eighteen-years old.

When the test came back that Tah was actually Malani's father, Tah gracefully took his daughter in. Tammy, who was Tah's mother, had flipped out when her son came home with an infant telling her he was the father. She was livid. After seeing Malani and her resemblance to Tah and herself,

Tammy warmed up to her and the thought of having her around.

One day when Tammy was out trying to cope some heroin from one of her favorite dope spots, she was arrested on drug charges. She spent eight months in the county jail, which helped her kick her dope habit. While Tammy was in jail, Tahiry and Phenom helped Tah with his daughter and five-year old brother, Travis. Tahiry had a job at Wendy's while Phenom was in the streets selling crack cocaine with Tah.

"Bismillaahir Rahmaanir Raheem, Qul A' Udhubi Rabbin Naas, Malikin Naas, Ilaahin Naas, Min Sharril Waswaasil Khannaas, Alladhee Yuwaswisu Fee Sudoorin Naas, Minal Jinnati Wan Naas," Tah recited in Arabic, chanting Soorah An Naas.

In English, it meant in the name of Allah, the most beneficent, the most merciful, say I seek refuge with the Lord and cherisher of mankind, the king of mankind, the God of mankind, from the evil of the sneaking whisperer who whispers into the hearts of mankind, from among the jinns and man.

As Tah stood in his closet offering Asr, which starts at mid-afternoon and ends at sunset, Tammy was walking into the apartment with Travis in tow. Travis had just been suspended from school for attacking his gym teacher, kicking him in his groin because he was too tall to punch in his face.

Tammy was upset about picking him up because that meant she had to leave her couch. It had nothing to do with him getting in trouble at school. The faculty was under the assumption she was mad because her child had assaulted his teacher, but that was far from the truth.

Tammy was also pissed because she had to get up in the middle of her daytime show, *The Wendy Williams Show*. It also cut into her drinking time. Since Malani had come into her life, Tammy had kicked the drugs but started drinking daily. Her favorite drinks were Bud Light and E&J VSOP Brandy. She would sit in front of the television watching show after show, getting drunker by the commercial.

"Take your lil' ass in your room and don't you dare turn n that TV or that PlayStation!" Tammy barked, sitting down on her green suede couch. She kicked off her grey Reebok Classics, reaching for her beer and cigarette all in one motion.

"Whatever," Travis mumbled, walking down the hallway toward his room.

"What?"

"Nothing, ma."

"That's what the fuck I thought 'cause I'll run smooth up in your shit," she yelled, causing Tahiry to step out of Tah's room with Malani dead on her heels. "Y'all lil' fuckas think I'm some kind of joke around this mu'fucka!"

"Tammy," Tahiry called out, sticking her head into the living room. "Tahiem is in there offering salat!"

"Gandma, daddy in here paying," Malani chimed in, mispronouncing words as she held on tightly to the doorframe.

"Hey, Lani. Come and give grandma some sugar," Tammy replied, ignoring Tahiry as she sat her cigarette down, holding her arms open for her grandbaby.

Malani stumbled towards Tammy with a huge smile on her face, revealing just how loved she was by the same woman raising hell at her son. One thing that couldn't be denied was the love Tammy her for that little girl. She was her everything and there wasn't thing she wouldn't do for her. Whenever Malani was in the same room with her, you saw a much softer and sweet side to her.

Though Tammy was not proud Tah had a baby at such a young age, she was thankful her grandbaby was there and healthy. Tammy knew Sandy was getting high when she was pregnant with her. A few times, even she got high with her. So she was extremely thankful Malani came out with no complications. She was truly a blessing.

"As salaamu alaikum wa rahmatullah," Tah recited with his head turned towards his right. He was sitting on both of his legs, his left leg under him, while his right leg remained upright. That meant peace and mercy of Allah be upon you. Both his hands were on his knees, and his fingers were spread open as he turned his head to the left. "As salaamu alaikum wa rahmatullah."

Tah pressed his balled up fist against his musalla, pushing his way up to a standing position. He turned and walked to the door, leaving his musalla where it was. When he stepped out of the closet, he spotted Travis instead of Tahiry and Malani. Travis looked up and greeted him, "As salaamu alaikum, Tah."

"Wa alaikum as salaam wa rahmatullah," Tah returned, removing his Islamic garbs before neatly folding them up. "What are you doing home so early?"

"Mr. Blue kept talking shit, so I kicked his faggot ass in the dick. I got suspended for a week."

"Damn, Trav. You only been back in school for two weeks!" he replied as Tahiry walked back into the room.

"Tammy gets on my nerves, yo. Word up!" Tahiry announced, holding her white Galaxy S2 in her left hand.

"Whose nerves doesn't she get on?" Travis replied, turning on Tah's PlayStation.

"Where's Lani?" Tah questioned, looking behind Tahiry for her shadow.

"She's in the living room with her *gandma*, watching *Ghost Whisperer*."

"A'ight, let's get outta here before either of them realize we're gone," he said, laughing at Tahiry's impersonation of

19

the way that Malani pronounced grandma. He then grabbed his burgundy New Era 59 Fifty Newark Brick City fitted off his dresser.

Travis shook his head as they quickly snuck out of the house without Tammy hearing them. this was something he did every time Malani had his mother's attention. The two of them walked out of the front door of the two-family house where he stayed, located on Madison Avenue in between 18th Street and 17th Street.

It was closer to 18th Street, about four houses down from the corner. They'd been residing for the past four years. Tah led Tahiry across 18th Street toward Clinton Avenue to wait for the number 13 bus, coming from Irvington Terminal.

***

Down on Chadwick Avenue

"What's in the bank?" Phenom asked as he held nine twenty-dollar bills in his left hand. He was amongst his peers on the corner of Madison Avenue behind building 100.

"It's umm," Doug started to stay, quickly looking down at the ground as he counted the money they had in front of them. "It' seventy-four in there."

"Stop it!" Phenom shot back, cockily.

Doug looked up at Phenom and shook her head. "A'ight, let's get it then."

Chadwick Avenue was crowded with people from one end to the next. From Clinton Avenue all the way back down to Madison Avenue, there were women, children, drug addicts, teens, drug dealers, and gang bangers.

Doug and the Chadwick Girlz, as they called themselves, were posted up on the corner where most of them lived the majority of their lives. Doug picked the dice back up and started shaking them in her right balled up fist as everybody looked on with anticipation. Phenom knew Doug couldn't really roll dice. He was just trying to come up off of her after he'd already won forty dollars from her and twenty-five dollars from Doc.

Doug stood there with a smile on her face, wearing a pair of light blue Seven jeans, a red short sleeve Galaxy t-shirt, and a pair of black on black Nike Air Max. Atop Doug's head was a red and black New Era 59 fifty New Jersey fitted, tilted to the side with much swag.

Doug favored a heavier tomboy version of the singer, Ciara. Even with the extra weight, Doug was still a cute girl in a rough shell. Doug was the oldest member of the Chadwick Girlz, and out of all nine of the members, she had the purest heart.

"I got twenty dollars that say Doug ace up again," China said, looking at each face that stood to her left and right.

"Bitch, you must be in the mood to be giving out free money!" Doug spat, tossing a twenty-dollar bill on the ground in front of China's feet while shaking the three dice in her left hand.

"Shit, let a bitch get in on that bet!" Jerm joined in, tossing two ten-dollar bills on the ground, as well.

"Hey, it ain't no fun if the homies can't have none!" Tabi laughed, pulling a stack of ones and fives out of her bra, itching for some of the betting action.

"Man, fuck that. Doug, roll the mu'fuck'n dice!" Phenom said, losing the little bit of patience that he had.

The Chadwick Girlz consisted of nine wild ass girls that thrived off doing everything that a dude could do, looking out for one another. There was Doug, Tabi, Liz, Vee, Doc, Tahiry, Mona, Lissa, and Chela. They were the young crew out there on Chadwick which the Bloods gave respect to because they went hard for theirs. And on top of that, they were buying work off of the big homie of the Bloods sect, GK.

Doug quickly released the dice against the step outside of the back door of building 100, which was on the corner of Chadwick and Madison. The dice beat against the wall as a black Dodge Magnum pulled right up on the corner undetected. The occupants of the Magnum were watching the dice game from behind the tinted windows. The Blood homies in the middle of the block slowly noticed the Magnum.

However, they thought nothing of it because dudes were always pulling up to the corner to holler at one of the girls. Fiends walked past with their minds stuck on getting high or coming up with a scheme to get high, hustling hard for that fix! Children ran rapidly throughout the block enjoying the years awarded to them to be a kid, jumping rope or riding their bikes in the street.

"Tracy!" Doug yelled, throwing her arms in the air after the dice landed on two ones and a three.

"I can beat a three with my eyes closed and both of my hands tied behind my back!" Phenom exclaimed, bending down to pick up the dice as Doug picked up her side bet money.

***

Around the Corner on Bergen Street

"As salaamu alaikum, Okhi," Mr. Studie greeted, sitting in front of building 100 as Champ stepped through the doors.

"Wa alaikum as salaam," Champ returned, looking across the street to his right at Lincoln Fried Chicken, which was closed. Turning his head back towards the front of him, he noticed a red Family cab pull up to the curb. "What's it looking like out here, Mr. Studie?"

"What can I say? It's the same damn Bergen Street!"

"Yeah, it's the same thing everyday and everyday we look for something new with no results."

"Rob, come help me with Mya so I can take these bags outta the trunk. This stupid mu'fucka wild'n!" Liz explained, standing outside of the cab holding the back door open. Champ could see little Mya sitting in her pink and black Gerber car seat.

"Damn shame them foreigners be acting like they better than everybody!" the older lady, Mrs. Baker, expressed. She was sitting on a dingy orange beach chair outside of the fence that surrounded the building.

"Shit, tell me about it!" Ms. Willis joined in, looking down through her eyeglasses.

"A'ight, here I come," Champ replied, knowing how the older women that sat in front of the building could get.

Sixteen-year old Robin "Champ" Bowman is what you called a venomous brain. He was mentally dangerous for his age and could be fairly dangerous with his hands. He stood 5' 4", weighing a 130 pounds with a honey roasted brown skin complexion. He had an I.Q. of 125, which was pretty high, the highest being 170.

It was Tah who started calling him Champ because of all of the *Scrabble* that he had managed to win over the years since he was about eight-years old. It was pretty scary how he was able to out spell men four times his age.

Champ wasn't street savvy like Tah, not exposed to them like he was at such a young age. However, Champ wasn't your everyday pushover. They were cousins through marriage on his mother's side, and one could say they were as close as brothers on most days.

Champ was originally from Millville, New Jersey, but at age seven, he was shipped up to Newark to live with his uncle because of the living arrangement with his mother. She couldn't afford to keep her child, so he stayed with her brother who didn't have any kids at the time. His uncle was married to Asia's sister, Trinice. Asia was Tah's, Uncle Squeezer's wife.

Champ walked over towards the cab as Tah and Tahiry came down the street from Clinton Avenue, so heavy in conversation since they'd left the house. He leaned into the cab and unbuckled Mya's seatbelt, wiggling her car seat towards him so he didn't lose his grip or footing.

Liz had just come from downtown Newark buying her and Mya a bunch of clothes with her welfare check. It was something that she did every month on the first, but her check came late this month. Liz was China's little sister, so no doubt did she receive the utmost respect in their hood.

China was the first lady of her Blood sect, surely a threat within a threat! Just as Champ sat the Mya in her car seat on the sidewalk, Tah and Tahiry stepped behind her. Tahiry then walked over to Liz to help her with her bags. Tah and Champ slapped five and embraced each other in a brotherly hug, something that they'd been doing for years now.

"As salaamu alaikum, cuzzo," Champ greeted him as they broke their embrace, looking towards Mya.

"Wa alaikum as salaam wa rahmatullah wa barrakatu," Tah responded, checking out the blue and white Jordan 12s Champ was wearing.

"Yeah, nigga! These joints are like that!" he said, reading Tah's mind once he saw where his eyes went to.

"When did you get thos—"

Boc! Boc! Boc!

Pop! Pop! Pop!

"What the fuck!" they all spat in unison, looking towards the back of the building where the shots came from.

***

"This nigga aced up!" Doc laughed after Phenom rolled a one and two sixes, failing to beat Doug's three.

"Shit, I should've been betting against this nigga," China announced as the front and back passenger doors of the Magnum flew open, releasing two masked gunmen.

"I wish you would've and then maybe I would've beaten the tracy!" Phenom replied, kicking the dice against the wall before turning around to the unraveling drama that unfolded. "Shit!"

"Nigga, you know what it is," the first gunman growled, pressing the cold steel of his .9 millimeter against the back of Tabi's head, causing her eyes to pop out of her head.

"A'ight, now let's all play nice and this will—" the second gunman tried to explain before gunshots were fired.

Boc! Boc! Boc!

Pop! Pop! Pop

"Aaggghhhh!" the second gunman screamed out painfully, his body dropping to the ground. The money he had in his hands flew into the air.

Phenom couldn't believe he'd been caught slipping once he spotted the two gunmen. His heart pounded rapidly in his chest knowing it only took one second for his life to quickly come to an end.

Seeing Tabi with the barrel against her head forced Phenom to react the only way he knew how. His palms were sweaty and his survival instincts quickly kicked into overdrive. The driver of the Magnum had caught him pulling his .38 out a little too late, but he still grabbed his .380, aiming it in Phenom's direction before letting three shots off.

In the blind as he tried to duck those shots, Phenom pumped two of his own into the second gunman, the third one hitting the back door of the Magnum. Everything was happening so fast, the first gunman was stuck there confused along with the Blood homies down the street.

It never registered to the first gunman to make a run for it because he just knew this would be a sweet lick. He had yet to pull the trigger to his .9 millimeter because he was still trying to fathom that his man was on the ground motionless.

In the midst of everything, Phenom was unaware that China was on the ground clutching at her chest from a gunshot wound. She was in so much pain, she couldn't even alert anyone that she was hit.

Just as the second gunman was about to check on his man, a bullet flew past his ear alerting him to the situation that lied ahead. He knew it was only a matter of time before the Blood homies ran up. With cat-like reflexes, he quickly dove for the Magnum, barely leaving the ground as he landed in the back seat.

The Magnum was able to pull away from the curb as the other two gunmen escaped with their lives through the skin of their teeth. Tah, Tahiry, Liz, and Champ came running around the corner towards the bullshit blindly. Liz had given Mya to Mrs. Baker to take into the building before she got hurt.

The Magnum made a wild left turn up Madison Avenue as the four of them reached their friends. Confused, they tried to see if everyone was okay. Still, nobody knew that China had been shot. The pain was so severe, she was unable to talk. All she could do was lie there, trying to breathe as best as she could.

"What the fuck!" Tah yelled, while Phenom stood directly on the corner holding his smoking .38 at his side.

"Is everybody okay?" Tahiry asked as the girls started to climb back to their feet as the Blood homies came down the block with their guns drawn.

"Them mu'fuckas had that fuck'n gun to my head!" Tabi screamed heatedly, tears doing a marathon down her cheeks as she stood up and faced Tahiry. Onlookers stood off to the side shaking their heads, not at all impressed with what just happened seconds ago.

"Oh my God! China!" Jerm yelled, being the first to realize she never returned to her feet.

"Somebody call 911!" Doug screamed, dropping to her knees once he noticing the small pool of crimson red stain on her pink and white short sleeved LRG t-shirt.

Tah and Champ were standing on the corner next to Phenom and the trio were all giving one another the look of obviousness, they knew that they were up to bat meaning it was up to them to rectify this situation.

Champ wasn't the gangster type, but he knew he still had to do his part. He kept his eyes on the business at hand, backing up Tah and Phenom with whatever they needed. Phenom, however, was just the opposite. He was definitely the nigga to get the job done at all cost. He wasn't book smart nor business savvy, but he could murder without a second thought.

Tah, however, was swift in all those areas. He was what most would consider a gangster and a gentleman. He was just the right dude to be in charge of something. The three of them stood there really not too sure of anything else other than the fact that it was on. China being shot wasn't something that could *ever* go unanswered!

Duquie Wilson

CHAPTER 2
10:23 p.m. That Night

"What the fuck are you waiting for, Tahiem? GK already told you what you needed to know about these mu'fuckas!" Liz barked, her eyes swollen. It came from all of the crying she'd been done that day, standing in Evergreen Cemetery in her black spandex maxi dress.

"Liz, relax. We need a lil; more information on the situation than just who did it," Tah replied, clutching his black iPhone 2S tightly, thinking about China who was laid up in the hospital undergoing surgery.

"Are you fuck'n kidding me right now!" she yelled as Doug put her left arm around Liz's shoulder. Liz shoved his arm away and took a step back before continuing. "My fuck'n sister is laid up in U.M.D. fighting for her gotdamn life and you're standing around talking about you need more than the names of who did it! Tahiem, what the fuck, nigga?"

"I'm on it, Beth. I said relax," Tah calmly told her, trying to keep from snapping on his girl.

"Fuck relaxing, nigga! You, Robin, and Greg need to handle this shit before I do!" Liz spat. She walked away, leaving Champ and Doug staring at Tah.

"She's right, Tah. With the son's picture and name being plastered all over the news, we don't need GK to confirm who the other two niggas are," Doug said, standing against somebody's headstone holding a bottle of peach Ciroc in her right hand. "All we gotta do is figure out how to catch up with these niggas."

"First of all, Greg is outta of commission right now, thanks to his carelessness. The whole Newark is looking for him. Secondly, the only thing that I'm sitting back and doing is trying to tame eight emotional ass bitches that wanna tell me how to move when I'm very well capable of thinking for my mu'fuck'n self!" Tah spat, hurt by the way Liz had just spoken to him. "And last but not least, I can't move on a mu'fuck'n soul until I receive an address, phone number, or fuck'n block to find them on! If I leave it up to y'all, I should be out on every block shooting at anybody until I'm either shot down or hauled off in fuck'n handcuffs!"

Doug wasn't at all shocked at the way Tah flipped out. He was known to spazz out from time to time. With China being shot and Liz going on a rampage, she knew he was under a lot of pressure.

Tah and Liz were now seeing each other openly. She knew by throwing herself out there to handle the situation, Tah would get a move on it. She knew there was no way he would allow her on the front line after everything that had just happened to China.

He was putting his all into finding the shooters and killing them. Bottomline, China was in the hospital fighting for her young life and her sister was out here lost without her better half. Liz didn't know what she'd do if China didn't pull through, so she chose not to think about her not making it.

Phenom was out in Hillside, New Jersey at his cousin's house. He was hiding out, learning he was wanted for questioning in the murder of the second gunman. As soon as his picture was shown on TV, he took off. His fingerprints were found on one of the bullets found inside of the dead gunman, so police wanted to talk to him. He knew that meant they were going to arrest him and quickly close the case.

GK, who happened to be China's big homie, let it be known he was going to paint the town red in search of the other two gunmen. He wanted Newark to know you couldn't touch any of their homies and get away with it.

Tah called a meeting in Evergreen Cemetery, which was right next to Weequahic Park. He wanted to break the news to Liz and Doug, but things didn't go the way he planned. Through the connections of his father's trusted people, he was about to have the whereabouts of the other two gunmen.

"What's our next move?" Champ asked, knowing Tah had a plan that would need his strategic and methodical thinking to ensure their success.

"I'm waiting for a phone call from Wheatie that'll point us in the right direction. Doug, I need you to stay focused on that other thing. You and Doc," he said, standing there in a black Sean John linen suit that Tahiry bought him. "I need the crew ready when it's time to move."

"And Liz?" Doug asked.

"I got Liz. Just stay focused on Doc and Tabi. This has to be as smooth as silk when it goes down."

"And what about, Greg?" Champ questioned, standing across from Tah as he stared off into the darkness. "He can't stay in hiding for too long. We need him out here."

"Call up a good lawyer. See how much it's going to cost to handle the questioning without them locking him up," he said, rubbing his temples with his index and middle fingers. He realized the task at hand was serious. "Doug, let everybody know we need to put something up for Phenom's lawyer."

"A'ight."

"I got two hundred for him right now." Champ informed him.

"A'ight, I'ma see what I can come up with in the next few hours, but y'all know that I'm limited right now," Tah replied shamefully, knowing he should have had more.

"Don't worry about it. Just take care of the China situation and I'll make sure that Phenom gets a lawyer," Doug said.

"A'ight, bet," he returned, closing his eyes to block out the reality of the world for just a few seconds.

***

8:43 p.m. The Next Night

"And you're sure these niggas live over here?" Tah asked, sitting in the driver's seat of a stolen tan Mitsubishi Galant ES. He had his black iPhone 2S pressed against his left ear.

"The address my peoples gave me is 19th and 22nd, so I know it's legit. Go there and I guarantee you you're bound to run into Dowe or Skip," Wheatie replied, sitting in his livingroom watching the movie, *Basic Instinct*.

"A'ight, bruh. Good looking."

"You know that I got you, lil' nigga. When's the last time that you spoke to your father?" he questioned, already knowing the answer.

"It's been a while, but he still writes me every month. I'm just not ready to forgive him for how everything went down, you feel me? He left us out here with nothing. He left me out here to fend for myself!"

"Tah, you could never be out here by yourself as long as I got breath in my lungs. But I understand how you feel when it comes to needing your father, so I'm not pressing you on that. Just know that Mujid wasn't the greatest man or father. However, he lived for you and your brother and I know he would love to hear from you."

"Yeah, a'ight. Look, good looking on the heads up on that other thing, bruh," Tah said, letting it be known he didn't want to talk about his father right then.

"You got it, lil' bruh. Hit me up later so we can hit the pool hall or something."

"A'ight, bruh."

Tah hung up on Wheatie feeling bad he came off like. He was still angry with Mujid for leaving him the way he did because his Uncle Squeezer had warned him to get out. But Mujid refused so Tah felt like his father chose the streets over him.

For the past five years, Mujid had been writing Tah and Travis a letter every month. From time to time, Mujid would call the house and speak to Tammy and Travis, but Tah refused to acknowledge his call. Wheatie was one of Mujid's soldiers that had just come home after serving four years in the Feds. He was charged with minimum charges because of his role as the delivery boy like Tah.

Tah and Wheatie had clicked after they met during one of their many deliveries. It happened rather quickly considering the circumstances. Wheatie was seven years older than Tah, but they were mentally on the same level.

He liked Tah because he reminded him so much of Mujid. A lot of the dudes that were now home after serving their time, were a part of Mujid's empire. They always lookedout for Tah out of respect and love for him, most of them being distant friends of Tah's.

Tah and Phenom sat inside of the Galant, which was parked on the corner of 19th Avenue facing 22nd Street, facing the corner store across the street. Phenom wore his navy blue Yankees fitted, pulling it down low over his eyes as he loaded his .38 revolver.

He was dressed in a Blac Label t-shirt, a pair of True Religion jeans, and a pair of black on black Jordan 11s. He was ready to dead the niggas responsible for shooting China!

Tah sat in the driver's seat holding a black chrome .9 millimeter, dressed in a black Champion sweatsuit. They both were wearing black baseball gloves.

Tah sat his S2 on his lap before reaching into his pocket and pulling out Beanie Sigel's *The B-Coming* album. He slid it into the CD player and turned it to track thirteen, which was China's favorite song, "Look At Me Now". It was a song she listened to everyday at least ten times. She was a beautiful person but a gangstress at heart fully.

"*My hair was knotty then Nose snotty then. Sweats, no pockets then. Facts? No problems then. News? Watchin' karate, and then Muddas playin' double dutch. She was hopscotchin' then. Me girl watchin' then. Crooked little eye, eye. Humpback, tryna hump that. Yes I, I. Couldn't play because I'm poo They thought I was mockin' them,*" Tah rapped. Closing his eyes, he thought back to the first time he'd heard China playing the song.

"*That movie was whack as hell!*" *Doug said, sitting in the passenger seat of the stolen gold 2008 Audi A6 wearing a brown Dickies one-piece jumper as China made a right turn onto Bergen Street from 16th Avenue.*

"*Nah, that shit was poppin'! You just wack as hell,.*" *she replied, lighting up a blunt of purple haze.*

"*Fuck outta here, bitch!*"

"*The movie was ass but Doug, you can be country as hell from time to time, my nigga,*" *Tah joined in, laughing from the back seat as China pulled up to the light on Springfield Avenue.*

"*You know what? Fuck the both of y'all! How about that!*" *Doug shot back as the traffic began moving through the intersection, before a white 2007 Audi S4 hit them from the back, grabbing all of their attention.*

"*What the fuck?*" *the trio barked, turning their heads around to the back out the window to see who just rammed them.*

"This bitch ass nigga" China laughed. relieved that it was her homie and not the police or the train, trying to force her.

"Who the fuck is that?" Tah asked, still looking out of the back window.

"It's my homie, Kodi," China answere, as the S4 pulled up next to them on the driver's side.

"What's poppin', mu'fucka?" Kodi greeted, leaning over the passenger seat of the S4, looking into the A6.

"What's Mob'n, nigga?"

"Tag, you're it," he laughed, before stomping on the accelerator and racing down 17th Avenue.

"This nigga play too much!" China laughed, following after him.

She realized she couldn't let the S4 get too far ahead of her. Doug and Tah sat back in their seats preparing for the car chase, not the least bit worried because China had the wheel.

Kodi raced past the precinct on the corner of Irvine Turner Boulevard, making it his business to snatch his emergency brakes. As he skidded around the corner, the tires screeched loudly.

China was hot on his bumper when he made a left turn. Unlike him, she didn't snatch her E.B.'s, her A6 slid around the corner just nicely. The two Audi's raced towards W. Kinney Street dipping in and out of traffic.

Kodi knew that China was going to bring it when he bumped her, but he was confident his S4 could out run her A6. While the S4 was skidding around the corner, China put The B-Coming CD into the CD player, preparing to make the right turn behind Kodi. The number 99 bus was sitting there on the corner, letting passengers board the bus as the A6 rocked onto W. Kinney.

Tah sat in the back smiling as the A6 drifted around the corner and down the hill. Kodi was rocking a right onto Prince Street by the time she reached the middle of the block, but she was hot on his ass while the lyrics played

"He busting your ass!" Tah pointed out, as the A6 swung onto Prince Street just in time to see the S4 rock a left down Montgomery.

"Don't worry about it. I'ma catch his ass," she replied, leaning forward to see the street better as he nodded her head to "Look At Me Now".

"Look, look," Tah sai, as Kodi made it look like he was about to turn onto Somerset. He threw the S4 into a 180 degree spin, now heading back towards the A6.

"Oh, he showing off right now on you, China."

"I see him, but watch this."

"What the fuck!" Doug gasped.

China snatched his emergency brakes, throwing the A6 to the left just catching the back bumper of the S4 as Kodi tried to race past them.

"There that nigga go right there!" Phenom informed, snapping Tah back to reality. He saw Skip walking out of the front door of the building, attached to the corner store.

"Huh," Tah blurted out, locking in on Skip who was wearing a white Galaxy t-shirt, a pair of Red Monkey jeans, and a pair of tan Timberlands. "Oh. A'ight, let's go."

"Wait, hold up!" Phenom ordered as Tah opened his door to get out and dead Skip. "Look."

"Oh, shit," Tah said, noticing the police officers that were closing in on Skip from all angles.

"This has gotta be one lucky ass mu'fucka!"

"He can run, but he can't hide. I'll get his ass in the Monster if I have to," Tah declared, letting his frustrations be known by the tone of his voice.

CHAPTER 3
Thursday
September 19, 2013
10:15 a.m.

"We declare that these united colonies are, and of right, ought to be free and independent states. That they are absolved from all allegiance to the British crown," Ms. Fairfell read aloud as she stood in front of her classroom with her teachers' history book open, her eyes glued within.

Tah was in class. However, his mind was elsewhere as he sat in the front row near the classroom door. Tah had his textbook opened to the page that Ms. Fairfell was reading like the other eleven students in the room, but his mind was on the China situation.

The issue had been weighing heavily on Tah, and the fact that Liz wasn't talking to him hurt even more. Word on the street was out that GK and the Bloods were out to avenge their homie. Still, Liz wanted the blow to come from her camp. She wanted Tah to settle the score for China.

With Phenom lying as low, Tah could only move at night which placed him in a tight spot. He didn't feel comfortable moving without Phenom because, truthfully, he'd never killed anyone before.

See, Tah used to be a runner for his father from the age of five until fourteen. He'd receive a package of drugs and was told where to drop them off at. The moment that the Feds kicked in their front door and folded Mujid's operation, Tah decided he would do his own thing.

The Chadwick Girlz, Phenom, and Champ all looked to him for guidance and leadership. Doug and Tahiry were the voices of the crew, as the girls sold drugs. Still, they all followed behind behind because he'd ran with a mean group of hard hitters. No one but Tahiry knew that he had never killed a soul, He'd shot plenty of people but never killed anyone. If he didn't body somebody quickly in the name of China, his crew would look at him differently.

"And all that political connection between them and the state of Great Britain is and ought to be totally dissolved. And that, as free and independent states, they have full power to levy war, conclude power... excuse me," Ms. Fairfell said. She pinched the bridge of her nose,continuing. "I mean, conclude peace, contract alliances, establish commerce, and do all other acts and things which independent states may of right do—"

Knock, knock, knock.

"Yes?" Ms. Fairfell answered, after she was interrupted from her reading.

The door slowly opened and everybody's attention in the classroom turned towards the door out of curiosity as to who was interrupting their class. To everybody's surprise, in walked two African American men in suits escorted by two Caucasian men in police uniforms and the principal, Mr. Hellburch. The man in the front of the convoy raised his badge, and said, "Good morning, Ms. Fairfell. My name is Sergeant Wright and this is my partner, Detective Maur."

"Ummm, good morning, detectives. What brings you to my classroom today?" she nervously asked, sitting her teacher's book on top of her desk.

"We have an arrest warrant for Tahiem Muhammad in connection to a murder," Detective Maur replied, holding the arrest warrant up in the air.

"A warrant? A murder? For Tahiem?"

"Yes, ma'am."

"Are you certain that you have the right person? I mean, Tahiem is a good kid and one of my best students!"

"We'll take that into consideration, Ms. Fairfell, but either way, Mr. Muhammad has to come with us," Sgt. Wright returned, locking eyes with Tah.

Tah was at a loss for words as the two uniformed officers approached him, causing his peers to whisper amongt themselves as he was cuffed. Being wanted for murder had ever crossed his mind, even after his father went down for running a drug empire and multiple homicides.

Tah knew damn well he hadn't committed any murders, ever! Once he was handcuffed, he lowered his head in the infamously traditional criminal fashion, taking the walk of shame out of the classroom and right out of Weequahic High School.

Principal Hellburch didn't say a word. He just allowed the police to come into his school and arrest one of his best students. The other students, as well as Ms. Fairfell, were looking to him for answers, but he lowered his head like a coward and walked out of the classroom. He didn't have any, honestly. He was just as nervous as they were in the detective's presence.

***

Across Town

While Tah was on Chancellor Avenue being arrested and stuffed into the back of a Newark Police squad car, Phenom was out doing the devil's work when he should've been in hiding. He was down on Irvine Turner Boulevard and W. Bigelow Street, sitting in a stolen brown Oldsmobile Cutlass. He was looking around the area peeping the scene, trying to stake out his getaway.

Greg "Phenom" Dickens was a nineteen-year old middle school dropout. He grew up extremely poor with no food to eat or a place to call home. Phenom, his two brothers, Boz and Rich, and his mother lived in one abandoned house after another as squatters. That's how Tah and Phenom actually met.

Tah had been kidnapped as a kid, taken for ransom, and dumped into the basement of an abandoned house on Chadwick and Hawthorne Place. He felt like his young life was surely over.

While the kidnappers were waiting for Mujid to respond to their demands, Phenom was in the basement freeing Tah from the rope that was tied around his wrist and ankles. He was Tah's savior that day and because of his heroic act, Mujid gave Phenom and his family a place to call home.

He'd paid the first two years up in rent in their apartment and gave Phenom's mother, Quisha, twenty grand. That day down in the basement, Tah had to trust that Phenom wasn't there to hurt him. In the midst of that, a bond was formed.

Now standing 5' 9", weighing 209 pounds, Phenom was anything but that little homeless kid in that abandoned basement. And the bond they shared after that night was amazing. They always had one another's back no matter the situation.

Climbing out of the Cutlass, Phenom put his left hand on his waist, steadying his .38, while using his right hand to close the driver's door. On his head was a dreadlock wig cap. He was dressed in a Ryder's moving uniform jumper with a pair of black Spalding baseball gloves on his hands.

He made sure he was seen by all of the people going about their day as he walked up to the gated three-family house. He did that by tripping over the garbage can that sat on the curb for the garbage man. Reaching the top step of the dark grey wooden porch, he made even more noise by whistling loudly.

He was setting the scene he wanted any potential witnesses to see and hear. He walked up to the front door and looked to his right at the doorbells where the tenants' names were located.

When he saw what he was looking for, he turned back around and headed back to the Cutlass. On his way down the walkway, his red Samsung Galaxy S2 began to ring. He knew it was somebody of importance because of the ring tone that was sounding off. It was The Script's "Break Even" ringtone.

"Yo?" Phenom greeted as he neared the Cutlass.

"Greg, where are you?" Tammy asked nearly in tears. She'd call him from Tah's iPhone he had left in the house that day by accident.

"Tammy?"

"Yeah, where are you?"

"I'm in South Carolina right now. Why, what's up? Where's Tah?" he asked, lying about his whereabouts as he wondered why she called from his phone.

"Tahiry just called me. She told me somebody told her that Tahiem was just escorted out of the school in handcuffs," she said as he opened the car's back door and grabbed the heavy duffel bag that was on the backseat.

"Handcuffs?"

"I need to know what's going on but I got Malani with me. I'm not taking my baby down to no police station."

"A'ight, stay by the phone. Let me call Tabitha and see where she's at. She'll come and get Lani so you can go check on bruh."

"A'ight, hurry up and call me back."

"A'ight," he returned, hanging up. "Shit!" he barked, banging his fist on the roof of the Cutlass.

Phenom dialed Tabi's number as he walked back toward the house carrying the duffel bag. He was walking inside of

Duquie Wilson

the front door when Tabi answered the phone. He told her everything that had happened with Tah and his need for to go and get Malani so Tammy could go check on him.

Once Tabi told him she was on her way, they disconnected the call. Phenom then climbed the flight of stairs of the three-family house enroute to the third floor. He leaned in and put his ear to the door so he could hear insid.

When he was satisfied, he took a step back and raised his right foot in the air. With all of his strength, he kicked the door in and stormed into the apartment. He knew where his target was hiding, walking in on the forty-eight year old, potbelly man who was nervous, trying to gather himself.

Phenom walked over to him, aiming his gun in the guy's face as he told him to get down on his knees. Phenom sat the bag down on the floor and unzipped it before pulling out a roll of duct tape. He quickly duct taped the man's hands behind his back, then laid him across the bed. Next, he went into the bag and pulled out a Phillips head power drill.

"Please, you don't have to do this!" the guy whined, trying to see what Phenom was doing.

"That's where you're wrong. I have to do this for my lil' brothers, you faggot ass rapist!" Phenom barked, walking up to the dude's head that hung off the edge of the bed. "I'm goin' make sure you don't put your hands on nann 'nother mu'fuck'n child in this life time, pussy!"

"Pl—pl—please, I'm b—b—begging y—y—you. Pleas—"

That was the last thing the guy was able to get out of his mouth before Phenom began drilling into the back of his head with the drill. The guy screamed for a few moments before death consumed him.

Phenom wasn't here to play with him or waste time. Now he had to find out what was going on with Tah. He knew he couldn't be out in the streets for too long being on the run for murder. Once he was sure the guy was dead, he packed his things back up and walked out of the apartment like he'd never entered. Back to hillside he went!

***

1:30 p.m.

"Mr. Tahiem Muhammad, son of the famous king pin, Mujid Muhammad Jr. I guess the apple doesn't fall far from the tree, does it?" Detective Maur said, sitting across from Tah. His handcuffed hands were folded on top of the table in front of him. "I'm just curious as to how a piece of shit like yourself doesn't have a rap sheet as far as the stretchmarks on that dingy ass little drunk bitch that you call a mother!"

Tah squeezed his eyes to narrow slits, while grilling Detective Maur demonically. He clenched his hands into skin-breaking tight fists, his veins protruding violently, but he kept his mouth shut. Sgt. Wright walked behind Tah and said, "Maur, I don't think that you should bring Tammy Holmes up at a time like this. Definitely not in the disrespectful manner that you're doing."

"Fuck that fuck'n alcoholic druggie bitch!"

"I said enough already!" Sgt. Wright barked, trying to play the good cop with hopes that Tah would bite.

"We've got a dead man downtown at the morgue and a young woman in the hospital fighting for her life," Detective Maur spat, opening the yellow folder on the table in front of Tah, showing him the crime scene photos. "And you're sitting here sympathizing with this piece of shit murderer?"

"Not everyone is guilty, Maur. You haven't even asked Mr. Muhammad if he was there."

"Because I don't need to! I fuck'n know his ass was there!"

"Would you please interrogate the kid rather than insult him?" Sgt. Wright spat, turning his head towards Tah. "Tahiem, tell my partner here that he's wrong, and that this is a huge mistake."

"Nah, he's right about two things, my mother is a drunk and *ex*-druggie," Tah confirmed, still staring through Detective Maur. "And, I was on Chadwick that day now that I think about it!"

"I knew it, you and Greg—"

"However, I wasn't the shooter," Tah said, cutting him off before he could finish his statement.

"If you weren't the shooter, then who was?" Sgt. Wright questioned, believing that Tah was foolish enough to fall for the good cop/bad cop act.

"Lawyer."

"Speak up, boy! We can't hear you!" Detective Maur barked, leaning forward trying to hear what Tah said.

"Lawyer!" Tah yelled, leaning forward in his seat, nearly spitting in Detective Maur's face as the word left his lips.

Tah knew there was no way hell that this interrogation was legit because he was a minor from watching *Law & Order SVU*, *Criminal Intent*, and *CSI Miami*. He knew his rights as a minor. There was no way these two veteran detectives should have been questioning him without a lawyer and his mother present even though they were just fishing for a lead.

Of course he knew they didn't have anything on him to charge him. They were barking up the wrong tree for real. Tah sat there wondering where Tammy was because he'd purposely told one of the students to tell Tahiry that he was being arrested.

If his message was delivered, knew without a doubt that Tahiry had called Tammy. So there had to be a reason Tammy wasn't down there right now. He was starting to get nervous about sitting there that long knowing a few dudes had disappeared in police custody. The last thing he wanted was to die by the hands of the police.

The interrogation room was small and cramped with a stale smell of stillness, that lonely slit of air in the room peaking the mountaintops. With so much tension in there, it felt hard to breathe, especially the longer that he sat. Then the color in Tah's face was slowly fading.

Detective's Maur and Sgt. Wright couldn't believe that he'd just lawyered up on them without being able to trip himself up, convicting himself. Detective Maur's face flipped down into a droopy sag, the hairs on the back of his neck stood up. His jaw tightened into a vise grip clench, releasing his fire spitting rage.

Wiping his lips, Detective Maur shook his head continuously while standing up. He was ready to charge Tah with anything and just ship him to the Youth House Detention Center. Tah watched as both detectives walked out of the room leaving him sitting there with deep empty thoughts, unsure of what could happen next.

He wrapped his right hand around left fist and squeezed tightly, causing his knuckles to crack. As his nerves began to completely unravel, Tah cracked the knuckles in his right hand with his left hand before standing up. Phenom was somewhere hiding with every cop in Essex County looking for him and here Tah was, down at the precinct being implicated, harassed, and pancaked with conspiracy. He was in for a ride of all rides!

"Mr. Muhammad, you are under arrest for possession of a weapon and resisting arrest," informed Lieutenant Ellen

Microsoft, who walked into the room looking like the actress Indira Varma. Detectives, Maur and Wright, stodd behind her in the hallway smiling.

"Weapon and resisting arrest?" Tah questioned, in disbelief of what he just heard. "You're kidding me, right?"

"Hardly, now please stand up," Lt. Microsoft returned, standing over him with her handcuff keys in her hand.

"This is some bullshit!"

CHAPTER 4
Wednesday
October 23, 2013
7:49 p.m.

"Time on my hands since you been away, boy. I ain't got no plans, no, no, no, no. The sound of the rain against my windowpane it's slowly, it's slowly driving me insane. Boy, I'm going down," Liz sang loudly along with Mary J. Blige on her classic hit "I'm Going Down" as her *My Life* album softly melted throughout the alpine speakers of Tahiry's new smoke grey Buick Lacrosse.

"Damn, bitch. It's only been a month. You need to get it together!" Tahiry said, while interrupting Liz's little *American Idol* moment as she made a left turn off 15th Avenue onto Camden Street.

"Whatever, Tahi. So what, I miss my bae. This month feels more like two years!"

"Nah, you're right. It has been mad different not having big head around," she returned, while looking at her rearview mirror, eying Malani and Mya. They both were sitting in the backseat asleep in their car seats. "Malani has been asking for him like crazy."

"Yeah, it seems like Mya can feel Tahiem's absence, also. She's been sitting at the front door with her jacket in her hand, holding the pink pony he won for her in Wildwood last year," Liz replied, tears slowly storming from her eyes and down her cheeks, balling her hands into tight fists.

"You know she's connected to him just as much as Malani. Tah's the only father Mya's had since she was born," Tahiry said, making a right onto 14th Avenue when she felt her S2 vibrating under her right thigh.

She grabbed her phone with her left hand, keeping her right hand on the steering wheel. She didn't have to look at the screen. She already knew who was assigned Avant's "4 Minutes" ringtone. Tahiry handed Liz her phone, and said, "It's Champ. Answer it."

"Hello?" Liz greeted after swiping the touch screen to the right, putting the phone on speaker.

"Yo, where's Tahiry?" Champ replied ignorantly, already knowing that it was Liz answering the phone.

"I'm right here. What's up?"

"Who you in the car with?"

"Why?" she questioned, making a left onto Bergen Street after sitting at the red light for a few seconds.

"Because I need to holla at yo' ass, why else?"

"Shut up. I'm with Liz and the babies."

"A'ight. Where y'all at?"

"Around, nigga! Damn!" Liz spat, while Tahiry pulled up behind a gold Nissan Altima at the red light on South Orange Avenue. "Why?"

"Mind your business, Liz," he told her, hearing the aggravation in her voice. "I'm on Munn and Central. I wanna know where y'all at cause I need to holla at both of y'all. It's important."

"A'ight. Meet us on 18th at the 99 Cent store." Tahiry told him, as the traffic started to move.

"A'ight, I'll be there. How far away are y'all?"

"Damn, nigga. What are you? The police or something with all of these damn location questions and shit!" Liz snapped jokingly.

"Give us like twenty minutes. We'll be right there."

"A'ight, hurry up."

***

Meanwhile on Watson Avenue

"Where the fuck is this nigga at?" Dowe snapped, looking at the screen of his white iPhone 2S. He was sitting in his yellow Chevrolet Monte Carlo SS, listening to Lil Wayne's "Hustler Muzic".

"I don't know," his little brother answered, looking up towards Bergen as the number 39 bus pulled up to the bus stop on the corner.

"I know you don't know, dawg. I wasn't asking you where the nigga was at. I was just venting."

"Oh, a'ight."

Dowe had been sitting in his Monte Carlo that was parked on Watson Avenue directly across the street from Peshine Street School. They were facing Bergen in between Peshine and Hunterdon Street. He was on his way to his baby mother's house to drop off his little brother when he got a call for an ounce of weed.

Besides driving his brother Skip around when he did his stick-ups, Dowe was a petty weed dealer, but swore up and down he was that nigga. He ran around Newark lying about how much weed he sold and the money he made on a day-to-day basis. He thought people bought into his lies, but he was only one that truly believed what he was saying.

Dowe was able to stay on his feet because his baby mother would always give him her welfare check on the first of every month. He would take that check and flip it. Now he was good at selling weed and flipping that check every month, but he couldn't save anything. He always blew his money on nonsense after giving his baby mother her money back.

She would take that money and tend to the things in her household because Dowe still at lived at home with his mother. When his baby mother wouldn't give him her check because she was behind in certain bills, Dowe would cash in her food stamps for cash to make a quick flip. There was shame in Dowe's game. If he didn't do that, he was out with his brothers, Eric and Skip, robbing hustlers. A scheme that came back to bite them in the ass as of recently.

"I'm giving this nigga five more minutes and then I'm leaving." Dowe said, as a dude on a ten-speed Huffy bike turned the corner off of Bergen.

"That must be him right there on that bike." Dowe's little brother announced, as Dowe's 2S began to ring.

"Nah, but this is him right here," he said, pointing down at his iPhone screen as the number flashed across it.

"Darrel!" his brother screamed as Dowe looked down at his phone's screen.

Hearing the urgency in his brother's voice as he screamed his real name, Dowe raised his head, looking in his direction instead of ahead of them. His brother was in sheer shock, frozen stiff and scared shitless, looking at the biker that stood in front of the Monte Carlo. His silencer-equipped mach-II aimed directly at the windshield.

Dowe's eyes finally followed his brother's eyes, which were full of tears. He was granted a split second of the view his brother saw before both of their hearts dropped. The biker squeezed tightly, pulling the trigger of the mach-11, sending countless slugs into the driver side of the Monte Carlo. Two bullets instantly smashed into Dowe's face as glass debris quickly soaked the confines of the Monte Carlo.

Blood splattered all over the interior of the Monte Carlo, leaving a painted picture for police to see and clean up. Dowe's body was fell to the right, covering his little brother, taking a parade of bullets to his torso for good measure.

The gunman stood on the bike with his finger on the trigger until the thirty round clip was empty, the nose of the mach-11 lighting up the night's sky. Cars driving by couldn't believe what was happening right in front of Peshine Avenue School.

Once the clip was empty, the gunman lowered the mach-11, grabbed the handlebars of the bike with his left hand, and peddled his way into traffic. Because of the Goku Dragon Ball Z mask, the face of the gunman couldn't be seen as he rode across the street, heading towards Hunterdon.

Dowe's little brother lied underneath his body covered in blood, shaking fearfully after what had just happened. He also ehad a bullet lodged into his left arm and right knee. People quickly climbed out of their cars once they were sure the gunman was long gone. Some had their phones out dialing 911, while others were filming the aftermath to post on Facebook, Instagram, and World Star HipHop.

A small crowd quickly formed around the Monte Carlo as speculators began to ask each oher questions about what just happen. It wouldn't be long before the story was twisted into ten different directions about what happened. Th

All the while, the gunman was riding up Custer Avenue pedaling faster than before. By the time he had crossed Chadwick, he'd ditched the bike and was power walking towards a stolen black Audi A4.

"Hurry up, nigga!" Phantom barked, hanging out of the driver side window.

"Do you wanna be the next one to get shot, mu'fucka?" Phenom asked, jogging around to the back door. "Y'all niggas must think it's a game or something!"

Duquie Wilson

CHAPTER 5
Back Up on Central Avenue

"Yeah," Champ said, answering his iPhone after hearing Freeway's "Free" ringtone. "Where are y'all at?"

"Pulling into the parking lot, we're in a—"

"I see you, I see you," he told Tahiry before she could finish her statement as Tahiry parked two cars down from where he was standing.

Tahiry climbed out of her Lacrosse wearing a pair of all black Mauri's, a pair of tight fitted blue True Religion jeans, and a black Galaxy tank top. She walked over to the 99-cent store where Champ was standing at. He'd just gotten off of the number 24A bus just moments before Tahiry had pulled up.

Champ stood there in a pair of brown boot cut JCME jeans, a white, orange, and brown Polo button-up, a pair of tan construct Timbs, and a custom made brown Philadelphia Eagles fitted. As soon as Tahiry him, they embraced in a hug, greeting each other., Then peeled apart to discuss why they needed to meet.

Liz wondered what was so important, too. She would've been right out there with them if the girls weren't in the backseat of the car, but she'd never leave them in the car alone. Even though Tah was locked up, Liz knew if he ever found out she did something like that, he would flip his wig.

"So, what's up?" Tahiry asked as a woman walked out of the store, carrying two hands full of bags with her three children in tow.

"I just spoke to Tah not too long ago. He wants to know how that other thing is coming along with Doc and Tabi. He said if everything is a go, then y'all can move out on it."

"Ain't nobody doing shit until he gets home, and you can tell him I said that."

"He said you would say that. That's why he said to tell you to do as he say and not what you want," Champ replied, smiling as two thick chicks walked into the store.

"We're not doing anything until his big head ass get out. We gotta get him out, so before we do anyth—"

"He'll be home next week on house arrest until he goes back to court, but he expressed the need to have things taken care of like yesterday."

"House arrest? House arrest for what? On what charges?"

"The conspiracy charges didn't stick, but they hit him with resisting arrest and a weapons charges," Champ replied, looking at Tahiry.

"What weapons? Tah didn't have no fuck'n weapon when they came and locked him up at school!" she barked angrily.

"I know. Look, it's all a bunch of bullshit to hold him until they find Phenom or Tah actually slips up and admits to a charge."

"Tell him I said to call me. I don't know why he hasn't called me yet."

"I got you. Just get on that other thing for him and I'll make sure to tell him to call your phone."

"A'ight. Tell him to hold his head up in there, and let him know I'm on the other thing," she said.

"A'ight. Hit me up as soon as you find out the intel on that. Let Doc know he needs it done like yesterday," Champ told her, giving her another hug before she departed.

"I'm about to go see China."

"Okay, make sure you give China my love. I know she could use it right about now."

***

1:13 p.m. The Next Day In The Green Monster

"In a news update, the man shot to death in Newark yesterday on Watson Avenue has been identified as Darrell Clouds, the brother of Eric Clouds, the man shot down last week on Chadwick Avenue. Both Clouds brothers had been rumored to be involved in a string of robberies. Detectives are trying to piece together the reasons for both deaths. Lead detectives have yet to give up any statements as to where they stand with both murders. However—"

"Yo, did you hear what the news said about that nigga Dowe?" Tah's cellmate asked as he ran in the cell while he was writing Liz a letter even though he did.

"Yeah, I heard it. I told you I already knew who it was before the police knew," Tah replied without looking up from the yellow notepad that he was writing on. "Once I find out what building that faggot ass nigga Skip in, he gon' get it, too."

"I told you I think the nigga is in lock up. My homie told me that the nigga was in building 3, but he popped off on somebody yesterday when he got off of the phone," Mu informed. "He must've got word about his brother getting killed last night. He probably figured he was next and wanted to go to lock-up instead of being around everybody else."

"Could be."

"What the fuck is you doing, nigga?"

"Nothing," Tah answered, tearing the letter off of the pad and folding it up. He stuffed it into the envelope that was underneath the notepad.

"I know you ain't over there writing no letter and you only been in here for a couple of days!" Mu clowned, looking over Tah's shoulder trying to see what he was doing.

"I said I'm not doing nothing! Why, what's up, bruh?"

"I'm just saying—"

"Don't just say shit. You do what you do and I'ma do what I do!" Tah snapped, hating that Mu was trying to mind his business. "You cool and everything, but we ain't friends. We're locked up. This shit ain't summer camp!"

"Yeah, a'ight," Mu returned, walking back out of the cell to get on the phone.

Tah sat there in a green khaki county uniform with bobo's on his feet. He had been in the Essex County Jail, which was called the Green Monster for a five days now. He didn't have a bail nor had he seen a public defender or a lawyer since he'd been there.

Champ told him that he'd spoken to a lawyer that was supposed to be getting him out on house arrest. However, he'd been there waiting for this ghost of a lawyer which never came to see him. Tah was getting angrier by the second.

He sealed up the letter, dipping his fingers in water and swiping them across the flap of the envelope. He walked out of the cell and dropped it off at the officer's desk. He then walked over to the phones and sat down, picking it up to call Champ. He looked around the dayroom before getting comfortable.

He had been waved up as an adult instead of being shipped to the Youth House. Tah wasn't worried because he was going to hold his own no matter where he went to. The phone rang four times before Champ answered. Tah had to wait for the operator to give her spiel before connecting the call.

"Thank you for using Global Tel Link."

"As salaamu alaikum wa rahmatullah, Okhi," Champed greeted him, once connected to Tah.

"Wa alaikum as salaam wa rahmatullah wa barrakatu, Okhi. What do you got for me?" Tah asked, getting right down to it.

"I spoke to a brother down at the Masjid and he gave me the number to a lawyer he said is winning right now. He said that he could get you off," Champ told him, hoping this news would bring some light to Tah's dark situation.

"Well, why hasn't he been down here to see me to tell me something, anything?"

"I had to get the money he was asking for. He wanted fifteen hundred upfront as a retainer's fee. So I had to take the money that Doug and them were putting up for Phenom and give it to him."

"A'ight, so again. Where the fuck is he?"

"He should be coming to see you—what's today?" Champ asked, not looking for an answer as he thought about the day of the week. "He'll be down there tomorrow. His name is Dustin Johnson."

"Dustin Johnson!"

"Hey, you know him?"

"Hell no, but his name sounds like he was raised right there on Chadwick with GK and them!"

"Look, beggars can't be choosy. We're working with what we can, so deal with it. Now, he says he can get you out on house arrest, so be thankful you'll be home sooner than later," Champ snapped.

"Yeah, a'ight. Did you tell Tahi what I said?"

"Yeah, and she said to tell you she ain't doing shit until you come home. I told her what you said, but she has her mind made up already and she's not budging."

"A'ight, good looking. You did your thing, bruh."

"Tahiry also said to tell you to call her phone. She doesn't understand why you been haven't called her."

"A'ight, I'ma call her right now. Good looking out, bruh. Shukraan jazilaan, as salaamu alaikum wa rahmatullah."

"You got it, my boy. Wa alaikum as salaam wa rahmatullah wa barrakatu."

CHAPTER 6
Friday
November 29, 2013
Up on Vailsburg Terrace

"Ken, what's up, cuz?" Pont greeted, sitting in the passenger seat of a red Mercedes Benz S550.

"Same ole shit. Tryna get to this dollar," Ken replied, standing on the deadend side of Vailsburg Terrace just off of Myrtle Avenue, along with his little crew.

"That's what I like to hear. How much you got for me?"

"I ain't got shit for you. The real question is what do you got for me?"

"You know me. If you got the money, I got what you need," Pont confessed as the driver handed him a blunt of sour diesel.

"I'm good right now, but if you run across some fire dope, hit my phone."

"Kay, let me get change for a ten," his brother Bru said, standing on their porch with two fiends.

"I don't got it."

"Where's Fitz?" Pont asked, looking around the block.

"He where he at. I don't keep track of no man," Ken shot back.

"Yeah, a'ight. When you see him, let him know I'm looking for him."

"Nah, you can call his phone and let him know that you're looking for him yourself. I don't work for the post office!"

"Yo, your mouth is gon' get you in some shit that you can't get out of," Pont said, wanting to get out and address Ken's mouth.

Ken pulled his shirt up exposing, his .9 millmeter and said, "Trust me, I ain't worried about shit. You better go try that shit on them niggas down the hill, nigga! I know you!"

"Yeah, a'ight. You make sure you keep that on you at all times."

"Trust me, if you catch me without it, you got every right to knock my shit off."

"Oh, I will!" he reassured, smiling devilishly.

"Be my guest."

"Yeah, a'ight, make sure you tell my aunt that I said what's up."

"I got you."

Pont rolled his window up as the driver pulled away from the curb. He always came up here to check on his little cousins. It was something he did daily. With the death of Dowe, Pont wanted to come check on his family to make sure that they were on point.

Pont was looking for Fitz because that's his little brother. Tito "Pont" Chavis was born and raised in the Vailsburg section of Newark. He was well known for putting his gun game down. Those that knew him knew that he was all mouth.

***

3:45 p.m.

"Tammy, where is Lani's clean clothes at?" Liz yelled from Tah's room, as she dug through all of the clothes that were piled up in the corner.

"I don't know. I think Tahi came and got them yesterday thinking that they were her dirty clothes," Tammy answered. She was sitting in the living room drinking a Lime A Rita watching *The Wendy Williams Show*.

"So, she has no clean clothes here at all?"

"Elizabeth, I don't fuck'n know. Go look in my room. She might have something in there!" Tammy snapped.

"A'ight."

Liz walked out of Tah's room and headed down the hall towards Tammy's room. She hated coming to Tammy's house when Tah wasn't around because his mother's mouth could get reckless. While Tammy didn't have anything against Liz, she just hadn't been much of a people's person ever since Mujid had gotten arrested.

No matter what a person said or did to or for her, Tammy wasn't in a smiling mood unless it was Malani. Liz walked into Tammy's room and started looking around for any of Malani's clothes. As soon as she stepped in front of the dresser, she spotted a letter addressed to her from Tah.

She picked the letter up to see if it had been opened. Once she saw it hand't been opened, she walked back out of the room and headed straight to the living room. Tammy was sitting there laughing at Wendy Williams who was going in on a group of celebrities and their outfits. Liz stepped right into the room and stood in front of Tammy's way.

"Why didn't you tell me that Tahiem wrote me?"

"Because I had better things to do. Now get your lil' funky ass from in front of my TV before I be in a jail cell right next to him for killing your ass for blocking my show!"

"How long ago did this letter come?"

"Girl, I don't know. Look at the damn envelope and get the fuck outta my way!" she yelled, shoving Liz to the right.

"Whatever. The next time he writes me, make sure I get the letter or I'm gon' break that dumbass TV and then you won't be so busy!" Liz barked, walking off with much attitude as she ripped open the letter, beginning to read it.

Liz,

As salaamu alaikum. I miss you so much. I never thought it was possible to miss someone that doesn't belong to you the way that I miss you! Word is bond. These past couple of months have felt like eternities away from you and my babies. This is a feeling I could never get used to. The niggas in here are clowns, they think being in here is like some sort of badge of honor and shit. Smh.

They got me bunking with this kid named Mu. He's from Lyons Avenue and Clinton Place. For the most part, he's a cool dude. The only thing that bothers me about him is he's Blood. So a lot of his homies be in and out of my cell. You know I ain't with that whack ass Blood shit. So when they come in, I step out just trying to keep my distance from people.

I've been offering salat five times a day as I should and making sure that I ask Alla, for his mercy in this situation. I've been heavy in my Qu'ran and when I'm not studying, I'm reading a hood novel. They have so many hood novels in here it's ridiculous. Shit, maybe these niggas come back for the hood stories! Lol.

I just got my hands on this book by the Okhi, Duquie Wilson. The title of the book is "Thick Like Quick". It's a short story, but so far it's a good read. The brother has a gift for real. I know him from the seeing him around town. I used to drop work off to him years ago, but I never knew he could write like that. He's talented.

How are my babies doing? Please kiss them for me. I miss them so much. Words could never truly express the way my soul has been calling for them. I miss sitting in my room watching them try to play the game, claiming the other one is cheating. I miss hearing their voices. I miss their touch. I miss waking up to their smiles. I just miss my babies, all three of y'all!

Champ keeps telling me that I'm coming home, so I might be home when you receive this letter. Shit, I hope I am! But if I'm not home by the time you get this, just know that I miss you and can't wait to feel your touch. Your ass better not be out there fuck'n with no other niggas either.

I don't wanna hear that 'I love you' shit. Bitches cheat on their nigga while he's home, so miss me with all of that shit. If I find out that you even out there holding conversations with niggas, I swear on Malani's life I'm done with you! I know this can be adventure on you with me being gone, but I promise you that I'm coming home sooner than later.

Just bear with me, Liz. I love you, baby, I've been thinking a lot about us and I think that I'm ready to make it official maybe. You know how I feel about relationships. I don't feel like a woman can be faithful to a nigga, especially when I don't even have my shit all the way together. As a Muslim man, I know that it's my job to take care of my family. So that's what I'm trying to do before I commit to anything as far as we go.

I'm trying to make it through this whole ordeal without stressing. That's why I haven't called you or Tahi. I know by me hearing y'all's voice, I'm gon' go through it more than what I already am. So please understand why I haven't called y'all yet. This whole thing is really taking a toll on me, but I'm masking my own pain extremely well.

On another note, how is China doing? Is there any progress on her condition? What is the doctor saying? Has that detective called you since I've been gone? If so, what is he talking about? Did he ask anything about me?

Don't tell that mu'fucka shit, baby. Just leave everything up to me. I got it That's my word, wallahi. I love you, Liz, I can't wait to get out of here and feel your lips against min., I miss the way those big ass lips feel wrapped around this dick. Lol.

Nah, for real though. I miss you, baby. You know you mean the world to me, right? Let me go. My cellie just walked in the room. I hope you got to see the news today. I told you I got things under control. I love you. Kiss my babies for me.

Love,

Tah

Damn, I love the shit outta this nigga, Liz thought to herself, folding the letter back up as tears slowly rolled down her cheeks.

CHAPTER 7
Monday
March 3, 2014
7:38 p.m.

"Mmmmmm, mmmmmm!"

"What did you say?" Phenom asked, standing next to the three-foot hole that he'd just dug up.

"Mmmmm, mmmmmmm, mmmm!"

Snatching the tape off the man's mouth that was lying on the ground tied up, Phenom asked, "What the fuck are you talking about?"

"Come on, Greg! Don't do this, son!" the guy begged, his arms tied behind his back with his legs tied together at the ankles. "On everything, I don't know anything about what happened to your brother."

"I beg to differ. See, what we have right now is a failure to communicate. I know you were there when my brother was raped!"

"I didn't want to do that to him. I was forced to do that shit. Trust me," he whined, trying to figure a way out of the mess he was in. "I didn't want to be there. He held me against my will. I swear!"

"Now, how can I trust you when you first said that you didn't have nothing to do with it? Now you're switching up your statement, saying you were held against your will," Phenom said, pulling a water hose from next to the house they were behind. "Answer me that."

"Please, Greg. I swear, I won't say anything to anybody about this. Just let me go."

"Oh, I'm not worried about that. You won't see the light of day to to say a word, let alone discuss this matter," he replied, sitting the hose down and pulling the duck tape back out of his back pocket.

"Come on, man. Don't fuck'n do this shit!"

"Nigga, shut up!" he barked, punching the guy in his mouth with a brute force.

Phenom ripped a nice size piece of tape off the roll, then grabbed the water hose and stuffed it into the guy's mouth. The guy was still a little dazed from the punch, but he was trying to keep Phenom from putting the hose into his mouth.

Phenom wildly punching him in his face until the man was unresponsive. Then he stuffed the end of the hose in his mouth and taped it in there, wrapping the tape around his head about seven times. He made sure to not cover his nose, too. Once the hose was secured, Phenom dragged the guy towards the hole that he had just dug up.

He then tossed his body inside of it, leaving his head sticking out. He then began to toss the dirt back in the hole. Afterwards, he walked over to the house and turned the water on before walking away. He didn't even bother to sit there and watch the guy drown.

The guy woke up as the water started running into his mouth. He was choking fast. He couldn't swallow the water fast enough. His eyes darted towards Phenom's back as he walked into the darkness. He let out a little chuckle as he heard the guy struggling to breath. He made his exit with his mind now on getting at Skip who was still in the Green Monster.

***

Friday
March 7, 2014

12:15 P.M.

"Shit, girl! Got damn!" Tah moaned, with his head tilted back. With his eyes closed, toes digging into the soles of his black mid-top Air Forces, his hands gripped tightly around Liz's slim 23-inch waist. She hungrily gyrated her hips, suffocating her pussy with Tah's dick, riding him reverse cowgirl style.

Tah had missed his replica of the beautiful singer, Keyshia Cole. He loved the fact that Liz's facial features mirrored every curve of Keyshia Cole's. She even had the gap in between her two front teeth like the singer before she got them fixed. Tah found that gap to be extremely sexy on her.

Liz stood 4'10" with a butter pecan skin complexion and long jet brown hair that naturally hung down to the mid drift of her back. At seventeen-years old.,Liz's body was amazing to clone to that of Lafayette, Louisiana's own lovely native model, Bri E. AKA Ms. Ma'am. She was half African American, half Brazilian, and Caucasian, her father was African American and her mother was half Caucasian and half Brazilian.

"Ooh, daddy. R—right, r—right th—there," Liz moaned out excitedly with her hands on Tah's knees. Her legs folded in half, one on each side of Tah's. Her knees were on the edge of his bed, head turned around towards Tah.

With her stiff-nippled titties bouncing slightly, she methodically and enticingly arched her back, raising her pussy up and down on Tah's murderously erect nine-inches. "P—pl-pl-please. Ooohh shit, m—mu'fucka. Please, don't s—stop!!"

"I missed this pussy so fuck'n much!" Tah admitted, sucking on his bottom lip, feeling thegrip of Liz's vaginal walls contracting viciously around his dick.

"Ooh, I know y—you did," Liz replied, closing her eyes while licking her lips seductively, as her warm nectar cover Tah's dick like a coat of liquid skin. "I kept it nice an, ooohh. I kept it nice and tight for you, bae. Got damn, boy. You feel so fuck'n good in this pussy!"

Liz was wetter than she'd ever been since fucking with Tah. It was always wet but after not seeing him or feeling his touch for more than two weeks, her body was yearning for him fiendishly. She was putting a hurting on the dick, forcing him to play nice in the pussy to keep from cumming quickly.

He wanted to relish distantly of the walls that he missed so dearly. However, when Liz leaned forward and grabbed her ankles, Tah completely lost his mind. He couldn't fathom the feeling that engulfed his being. Liz's pussy had opened up just enough to suck Tah's dick in whole as she braced herself for the pleasing pain to come. Tah hungrily slid seven inches inside of her, ramming his head into her g-spot causing her toes to curl.

Without lifting her body an inch, Liz grinded steadily and slowly on the dick, giving them both unquestioned pleasure. In West Indian style swirls, while rubbing her clit against the length of Tah's thick vein popping shaft. She could feel the head of Tah's dick throbbing with pulsating blood rushing force.

As she spread her ass cheeks wide, she lifted her body up just slightly, and jammed her pussy back down onto Tah's dick. It was the right pressure needed to burst his pipes. Tah sat up and wrapped his arms around Liz's waist, gripping on to her in an intense and passionate bear hug.

"What the fuck!" Tah growled, preparing to pull his dick out of her pussy as he painted the top of her ass cheeks with his semen.

"Uh uh!" Liz yelled, forcing her pussy back down onto his dick, still swirling her hips hungrily. "I want you to cum in your pussy, daddy!"

"L-L-Liz,"

"Cum in your pussy, bae. I need to feel all of you inside of me," she seductively whined, tightening her vaginal walls even tighter around his dick in a suction manner. "Cum in your pussy, boy."

"Liz, w—we...shit," Tah moaned as the avalanche began, causing him to pump harder into the belly of Liz's pussy, tightening his grip around her. "Aaggghhhh!"

Now it was Liz's turn to bite down on her bottom lip as Tah's warm semen filled her insides, mixing in with her flavorful nectar. Although she didn't get to cum, she was so content at that moment, all she needed right then was to see a smile on his face that she gazed at.

The whole time that Tah was locked up Liz blamed herself for him being in there, with all of the murders that were happening as of late Liz had no real idea as of what she'd pushed him into doing. To see that Skip's little brother was murdered just days after Skip was locked up, Liz knew without a doubt that Phenom did it and Tah gave the order from jail.

Liz had screamed at Tah the night they were in the cemetery, telling him to kill in the name of her sister, and that's what he was doing. She didn't know how far he'd planned to go with this whole thing because bodies were still popping up everywhere around them, people she found herself not knowing in one way or another.

Lying back on his bed, her chest heaved up and down from heavy breathing when Tah said, "I can't believe you just—Yo, I cannot believe that we just did that! What now? What if you really get pregnant?"

"If I get pregnant Lani and Mya is gon' have a brother or sister!" Liz replied seriously, spinning around on Tah's semi-erect dick without releasing him from her pussy. She laid down on top of him, pressing her head against his chest. The crown of her head was underneath the cradle of his chin. "Tahiem, I've been thinking tha—"

"Thinking is a good thing. Thinking is the master key to success," he told her, while running his right hand through her sweaty hair.

"I'm serious, bae. These last six months were hell on me and Mya, not just Malani."

"I know me being away from the three of y'all is what hurt me the most. Not being able to see y'all faces was the end to all beginnings," he confessed, looking deep into Liz's eyes.

"Tah, I want you to move in with us. You and Malani," Liz blurted out, lifting her head off of his chest. "Mya needs you there in her life every day, every morning, every night. She needs her lil' sister with her twenty-four seven, three hundred and sixty five."

"Elizabeth Kimbrough, are you asking me to be your boyfriend?" Tah asked and smiled, looking at her as he saw the urgency in her eyes.

"Yes, nigga, I am!"

"And you're really serious about this?"

"What do you think?"

"I can be a handful, Liz. You sure this is what you want?"

"Nigga, I just let you cum inside of me. Yes, I'm serious and I'm sure this is what I want and need."

"Yeah, you did just let a nigga bust all in that wet shit."

"Well?"

"Liz, I've been your boyfriend for almost three years now. I wouldn't have it any other way."

"I know that already, but am I your girlfriend? Are you gon' let the world know that I'm yours?"

"Now you know that all of this shit is mine, girl!" Tah shot back, grabbing Liz's ass cheeks with both of his hands, squeezing each check playfully.

"Yeah, a'ight. You better start claiming me and not just Mya as yours, or somebody else just might be getting a taste of all of this tight wet pussy!" Liz said, squeezing her vaginal walls around his dick, causing his dick to began to come back to life.

"Yeah, a'ight. Don't fuck'n pay with me Liz. I'll be back in the fuck'n monster for murder one for real this time!"

"So, then you're going to move in with us?"

Tah let her ass go and wrapped his arms around her body. He looked up to the ceiling and said, "Let me think about it for a few days."

Duquie Wilson

CHAPTER 8
Wednesday
March 12, 2014
4:55 a.m.

"So, your source said that he's in there?" asked Detective Maur as he sat in the passenger seat of the unmarked burgundy GMC Envoy LS equipped with the Hemi.

"There's only one way to find out," Sergeant Wright returned, picking up the police radio that was sitting on his lap as he sat in the driver's seat of the Envoy. "All units move in, and remember the suspect is armed and dangerous."

The morning was innocently still and quiet on 16th Street and 19th Avenue. The sun had yet to set and the birds had yet to sing. Sergeant Wright had received information from a source that had seen Phenom enter the apartment building in the middle of the block. This was the tip that they were looking for. There were six unmarked vehicles scattered throughout the block with six more on the block over just in case he tried to make a run for it.

Detective Ronnie Maur stepped out of the Envoy standing 6' 2", weighing 180 pounds. Detective Sergeant Sam Wright, shorter and a bit more heavier, climbed out standing 5' 9", weighing 210 pounds. Both were wearing nickel-plated steel Teflon bulletproof vest with their police badges swinging around their necks.

"All units in position," Sergeant Wright ordered on his radio standing beside the Envoy, holding his 11-shot chrome black .40 caliber at his side.

"I bet you he never thought we would find his ass here!" Detective Maur said, laughing as the officers surrounded the four-story building from front to back.

"All units in place, detective," said the officer, standing near the front door as he held his radio to his mouth.

"Copy that," Sergeant Wright returned, looking over at Detective Maur before proceeding towards the house quickly. "Yeah, but I bet you his ass will be shocked when he sees all of these guns we brought for his ass!"

* * *

Is my mind playing tricks, like Scarface and Bushwick
Willie D, having nightmares of girls killing me
She mad because what we had didn't last
I'm glad because her cousin let me hit the ass
Fuck the past, let's dwell on the 500SL, the E&J and
ginger ale

"How many more nights are you going to be out there doing God knows what while my dumb ass is sitting here wondering if you're dead or cornered off by the fuck'n police?" Stacie questioned as she stood in the bathroom doorway, while the Notorious B.I.G.'s "One More Chance" played loudly on her sound system in the living room.

"What's the matter? You worried about a nigga?" Phenom returned, smiling as he scrubbed his skin roughly with the soapy green washrag as he stood in the shower looking at Stacie.

"No, I just like staying up until six in the morning knowing that I have work in the a few hours!" she snapped, standing there with both of her hands on her hips.

"Well, in my defense, it's Saturday and you don't have to be to work until noon. Plus, it's not six o' clock. It's only like five fifteen, if that."

"That's not the fuck'n point, Greg!"

"Yeah? Well, get to the point already," he told her, turning his back so he could rinse the soap off. "I'm tryna enjoy my fuck'n shower!"

"The fuck'n point is your stupid ass is wanted for murder and you're out there in the streets like you can't be fuck'n seen!"

"Why don't you just go ahead and dial the crime stoppers hotline and tell them where the fuck I'm at!"

"Don't be fuck'n dumb! Why the fuck would I do some stupid shit like that?"

"You might as well, standing there screaming that I'm wanted for a fuck'n body like these dumb ass walls ain't thin as shit!"

"Boy, please. Can't nobody hear me through these walls with that shower running," she replied just seconds before they both heard a knock at the front door.

They both froze as they looked at one another, hearing the knock at the door. Both of their heart rates quickly shot through the roof. As Phenom looked around the bathroom, he realized that he'd left his gun in the bedroom. He had to make it to his gun before Stacie answered the door.

He had promised himself that when the time came, he was going to out just like 50 Cent. Not Curtis Jackson, but the real 50 Cent! The real 50 Cent, Kelvin Martin, was Phenom's idol and hero. He was and still is the only gangster to shoot it out with the NYPD in a project apartment and get away with it.

The man not only terrorized the streets but he single handedly took on the NYPD, both on the street and in the courtroom. He shot at several police in a shootout, then turned around and beat the charge in court! Phenom may have looked like the talented rapper by the name of Ransom from Jersey City, New Jersey, but he wanted to be just like the real 50 Cent.

As he turned the shower water off, Stacie walked out of the bathroom to answer the door. She didn't know what to expect at 5:20 in the morning other than the police. Phenom had quickly climbed out of the shower and rushed into the bedroom, grabbing his gun first, and then a pair of jeans.

The idea was to lay low until Tah could get him a lawyer to walk him in for questioning. Then the money they had for him had to go to Tah to get him out of jail. Still, Tah told him he had plans in motion to get him the best defense lawyer. Phenom knew he would because his brother had yet to let him down.

Phenom had been staying at his girlfriend Stacie's apartment, because somehow or another, the police learned he was crashing at his cousin's house in Hillside. It was getting harder and harder to hide out. Especially when he went out at night to either make money or put in some work, so his face was still being seen throughout the streets.

Standing at the bedroom door, he peeked his head out looking towards the front door. He pulled the hammer back on his .38 revolver, making sure he was ready. Stacie reached the front door and looked out of the peephole, but she couldn't see anything. There were two shadowy figures there, but the darkness of the hallway made it hard to see.

She slowly put her hands on the door and with a nervous pitch in her voice, she asked, "Who is it?"

"It's Newark Homicide, ma'am. We have a search warrant. Please open up the door," Detective Maur replied, holding the search warrant up to the peephole. "We have reason to believe that you are housing a murder suspect in your house."

"I'm sorry, but there's no person in here wanted for no such crime," she returned.

"Please, open up the door or we will be forced to kick it in."

"I'm not opening a damn thing for you or nobody else!"

"Miss, we have a warrant which states that you have to let us inside of the premises. Just open the do—"

"I don't give a fuck if you had Barack Obama and Hillary Clinton with you! I'm not opening my mu'fuck'n door for nothing!"

"Okay," Sergeant Wright responded calmly, turning towards the six officers that were hiding on the steps holding a batting ram. "Kick it in."

The officers quickly climbed the stairs positioning themselves directly in front of the door. They were trained for situations just as such. The hallway was rather small and dark, burning with the scent of piss, liquor, and weed smoke like your average smelling hallway in the ghetto.

It was extremely stuffy inside and the smoke detectors kept squeaking every three minutes. The situation was one of many the officers had invaded before. Detective Maur and Sergeant Wright both stepped to the side with their guns held high, aimed at chest level as they were prepared to shoot, if necessary.

The first two officers raised the batting ram high in the air, gripping it tightly as two other officers assisted in the measuring of the ram with the locks. Sergeant Wright held up his left hand, raising three fingers and began to countdown. He did this silently.

Once his three fingers were down forming a solid fist, he nodded his head, giving the go ahead signal. The officers swung the batting ram backwards and with the momentum of their bodies, they swung the ram into the doorknob and locks. The force from the batting ram not only forced the door open, but it took the entire door off the hinges, taking the frame along with it.

* * *

"What the fuck!" Stacie screamed angrily as her door came flying open.

"My bad, sis. Where's Greg?" Doug laughed, stepping into the apartment after shoving her way in forcefully with Champ in tow.

"Why are y'all playing so damn much!"

"We thought it was Greg behind the door trying to act like you," Champ answered, closing the door behind himself.

"Where is he at anyway?"

"He's in the bathro—"

"I'm right here. What's good?" Phenom answered, cutting Stacie off as he stepped into the living room with his .38 in his right hand.

"Who did you think was at the door?" Champ asked, spotting the gun in Phenom's hand.

"Y'all knocking on the door and barging in this mu'fucka at five in the morning like y'all the fuck'n police. Who do you think we thought was at the door?" Stacie shot back, taking a seat on her couch as her heartrate began to slow down.

"My bad," Doug told her, seeing how nervous she was.

"Shit, the whole fuck'n building heard y'all."

"We said our bad, nigga. Damn!" Champ snapped, looking at Phenom who challenged him with his eyes.

"What the fuck do y'all want anyway?"

"Tah said that it's going down tonight. He needs you to be on point cause Tabi's not going no more. It's me, you, and Champ," Doug answered. Stacie stared at the trio as if they were all crazy.

"Champ?"

"Yeah, me, nigga. You got a problem with that?"

"You ain't 'bout this life. This ain't scrabble, nigga!"

"Fuck you, Phenom."

"Sensitive ass nigga," Phenom barked, turning around to walk back into the bedroom. "Tell Tah to call me. This ain't gon' work."

"Whatever," Doug replied, looking from Phenom to Champ. She shook her head at how they treated one another from time to time.

* * *

After searching the entire building from top to bottom, Detective Maur was full of anger and rage. He looked at his partner and shook his head from left to right. He wasn't just mad because Phenom wasn't in the apartment. His partner had taken them on a wild goose chase and now they owed this woman for knocking her door off the hinges.

She could go down to City Hall and make the biggest complaint against them. Not only was Phenom not in there, but there were no traces of him ever being there! Sergeant Wright's source had them chasing ghosts and looking like idiots in front of their entire team.

So far, all that they had learned today was what not to do. The others stood off to side laughing at both of them. The team was back to square one on finding Phenom. He was clever enough to not be anywhere that they had been searching.

Detective Maur had to really sit back and try to figure out where to go next. They had a killer on the loose and bodies were continuously piling up every day. Sergeant Wright was ready to hunt down his source and see where they had gotten this information. He was so pissed they'd ran into a brick wall because of his sources.

CHAPTER 9
Later That Day on Osborne Terrace

"Where the fuck is my money, nigga?" Soo questioned as Pont and Tost held the young hustler upside down from the building on the corner of Tillinghast Street.

"Man, I told you already. I was gonna pay you this Friday. My girl gets paid then."

"Did he give your girl the shit or did you openly take this man's shit and dip off with his money?" Pont questioned, ready to release the kid's leg.

"Soo, I swear on my kid's lives, I'll have your money come Friday! Please!"

"So you think tmy time is dictated on when you're ready to pay me, huh?"

"Nah, I just figured that you would underst—"

"Drop is ass!" Soo ordered, turning around to walk away.

"Please, don't! I swear—" the kid pleaded before Pont and Tost let his legs go. "Aaaahhhhhhh!"

"Now that's how you take the trash out!" Pont laughed, walking away from the ledge.

The kid's body fell four stories, hitting the railing at the bottom that led to the basement. His neck snapping instantly, blood splashing in every direction. Soo walked away lighting his cigar without a second thought as to what had just taken place. He was getting used to this shit all over again.

Rasool "Soo" Melvin was the man in charge of an elite drug empire and even though he was in charge on the streets, he was still second in command behind Jahad. Jahad was running his empire from prison on the low through Soo since he was sentenced to life in prison.

Soo was Jahad's lifeline to the outside world. He made sure that Soo was lived wonderfully at the age of 41 and Soo honestly couldn't complain. Jahad was a part of something that he just couldn't walk away from, even if he wanted to.

There were plenty of times when he wanted to reach out and take care of his family, but his higher ups made it clear that he didn't exist anymore other than to make them money. Soo was born in Newark and grew up on 19th Street and 19th Avenue but couldn't stay out of prison. He'd just finished a fifteen year prison bid a little over a year ago.

While Soo was locked up, his little brother had been running with a few people that put him in position to pass something down to his big brother. His little brother was serving 500 months in the feds. Soo couldn't thank his brother enough for plugging him in with Jahad because he needed that.

He came home to more money than he had ever seen in his life and he was worth a smooth two million dollars. He was running multiple businesses for Jahad and moving even more drugs than Jahad did when he was home. Jahad was a part of a very powerful organization, and there was no way he could get out the group except being stuffing a pine box. Death was the key to their oath. Soo wasn't a part of that society even though he wanted to be. He was just the front man on the streets for Jahad because he couldn't be there.

A small crowd began to form as Soo stepped out of the building nonchalantly, headed towards his white Lincoln Navigator. Pont and Tost came out of the building laughing and conversing, keeping their guilty expressions hidden from the world.

Soo climbed into the SUV and continued watching *In Living Color* that was played on the 7-inch screen that was hanging from the ceiling. It was a show he watched every chance he got. Pont walked around the SUV and climbed in the backseat near Soo. Tost climbed into the passenger seat, still laughing at the way the kid screamed on his way down.

* * *

7:35 That Night

"How many niggas did Tah say was up in there?" Phenom asked, sitting in the backseat of the royal blue rental Buick Regal LS.

"It's three niggas in there other than Doc. She's not on the clock but she's do—"

"Man, I don't care about all of that!" Phenom snapped, cutting Champ off as he shoved bullet after bullet into the magazine of his new .45 desert eagle with the extended clip.

"Relax, Greg. It's not that serious," Doug jumped in, sitting there holding her chrome glock .380.

Doug knew that Champ and Phenom were beefing about how they'd rushed into Stacie's apartment yesterday. Stacie had been cursing him out about it. She didn't find anything remotely funny about Phenom's situation. She figured none of his friends should have the time to clown around about it either.

They argued about the situation for a few minutes before they had wild make-up sex. After that, Phenom had time to think about it and realized that she was right. When he said something to Champ about it, Champ tried to make fun of her. That's when they got into it.

"He good, trust me. And you, Greg, don't wanna go there with me again," Champ shot back, looking in the rearview mirror at Phenom.

"Hhmmph!" Phenom huffed, choosing to leave the situation alone for now.

The last time Phenom had tried to disrespect Champ to punk him, he called Phenom out for a fair one-on-one in Tah's backyard. Of course Phenom didn't turn down the fade and they ended up fighting. Champ got the best of him that day, feeling like he could take him at any given time now.

Champ was calm, cool, and collected, but he was far from a push over. He could throw down when it came to his hands. Phenom was serious with the hands too, but that day Champ had gotten the best of him.

However, over the years, Phenom was up on him when it came to their fights. Phenom was up one on Champ and Champ was one up on Tah. It was something they did more often when they were younger, but fought less as they got older.

Phenom was pissed off Tah had even sent Champ on this lick instead of Tabi as planned. He didn't feel Champ was built for this type of thing. This was the lick that Tah and Doc had been planning for a while now, and with Doc's help, he finally had everything he needed to make it happen. This was a lowkey work and stash house for a major pusher. Tah didn't know who the spot belonged to, but in the end, he really didn't care.

After everything Doc had told Tah, he had estimated there to be about $200,000 worth of money and drugs inside, a lick well worth hitting. Tah really no longer desired to be mixed back up in the life after what had happened to his father, so him, Phenom, and Doc would do licks to help put money in their pockets.

Tah knew right off the top he wasn't about to go on a long binge not selling whatever drugs he came out with. He was going to move that work and that was it. He knew all too well what this life could do to you, so he was hitting this thing with a blueprinted plan. He was about to set the tone for his future.

Tah had Tahiry were looking into all types of investments he wanted to jump into. He wasn't about to pick up where his father left off.

> *We still hustle till the sun come up*
> *Crack a forty when the sun go down*
> *It's a cold winter*
> *Y'all niggas better bundle up*
> *And I bet it be a hotter summer*
> *Grab a onion just to lock it down*
> *You hot now, listen up*

"Yo, turn that shit the fuck down!" Phenom barked after Champ turned Freeway's "What We Do" featuring Jay Z and Beanie Sigel up higher than it needed to be.

"Word, you wild'n right now, bruh!" Doug jumped in, shooting Champ the coldest stare.

"My bad. This my shit. I forgot where I was at for a second."

"This why I fuck'n told this nigga that this was a bad idea," Phenom said, shaking his head with disappointment.

"Well, we here now and we gotta work with what we're working with," Doug told him.

"Look, we gon' run up in there, dead everything, and be—"

"Hold up. When you say dead everything, you talking about killing everybody up in there?" Champ asked, shock written all over his face, looking towards Doug for confirmation.

"Congratulations. Somebody get this mu'fucka a Scooby snack for catching on so gotdamn easily!" Phenom clowned as two teenaged girls walked past the Regal LS. "Doug, as soon as we get in between the houses, pull this bitch around the corner. This ain't gon' take but five minutes tops and we'll be coming out."

"A'ight, say less," she replied, looking in her mirror as a red Family cab rode by headed toward Avon Avenue.

"This is some bullshit!"

"Nigga, shut up and bring your ass on!" Phenom ordered, opening his door and climbing out.

Phenom quickly jogged in between the two houses that sat in the middle of the block, carrying his .38 and his .45 down at his side. He was draped in his black Carhartt one-piece overall jumper with a pair of black leather Timberlands. He was ready to get down and handle his business at all time.

Champ hopped out of the Regal LS looking back at Doug. He was trying to see if she would give him any indication that what Phenom said was the truth. He didn't want any parts of anyone's murder. He looked from his left to his right nervously, before following behind Phenom. He was silently cursing Tah out for sending him on this wild goose chase with Phenom.

Champ was wearing a pair of blue Rocawear jeans, black G-Unit low top sneakers, and a black fitted. He refused to wear his good clothes for this. They both pressed their back against the outside of the house and waited for Doug to pull off before proceeding. Everything had to go as planned.

Tah had timed everything down to a T, so Phenom knew he couldn't waste a blink of a second. That's why he wished Tah would have never sent Champ.

There was another group of guys in the house across the street from the workhouse. This was the house the workers sat in when they weren't on the clock. Whoever was running this workhouse had his workers pulling 72-hour shifts at a time. So, when they weren't bagging up or counting money, they were across the street waiting their turn.

Tah knew when the bulk of them went across the street for their ten-minute break, so Phenom and Champ had less than ten minutes to get in and out. This was Champ's first time really deep in the mix of things. Needless to say, he was so nervous that he was shitting bricks.

First, he didn't have a gun, so he had to depend on Phenom and that didn't sit too well with him. Then he really didn't like their odds against all of the dudes Doc had told them were surrounding the house. He did, however, know that Phenom was a sharp shooter like Bruce Willis in the movie *The Last Man Standing.*

They both ran to the back of the yard and hopped the fence that separated 10th Street from 11th Street. They scanned the whole backyard before making a move towards the house, knowing someone could've been back there just hanging out.

Phenom led the way with both of his guns aimed high, ready to put a bullet in any and everything that stood in their way. Champ's heart was racing a mile a minute as they neared the back door. They pressed their bodies against the house and took a deep breath.

Champ looked up to the bathroom window that Doc left unlocked before they got there, leaving a ladder right underneath the window for them to climb up on. These were the exact plans Tah had mapped out, Doc following every detail down to the very last scribble.

Phenom started up the ladder first, skipping every other step. He was so anxious to get in, literally living for this type of shit. Champ was hot on his tail, promising himself that if he made it out of this alive, he was never doing no shit like this again.

As Phenom neared the window, he heard one of the dudes walk into the bathroom and close the door. Champ ran right into him when he stopped where he was. Phenom was right at the tip of the window, peeking in. He looked at the dude's back as he released his bladder which was full of Coronas.

Phenom wanted to shoot the kid in the back of his head right there but knew that wasn't a part of the plan, so he had to wait. To an excited and anxious Phenom, it felt like the kid was pissing from hours. It took him two minutes to piss. This nigga had the bladder of a racehorse! Without washing his hands, the kid walked back into the living room, leaving the door halfway open instead of closing it back the way it was.

Once Phenom and Champ crept into the bathroom having to be extremely careful, they crept towards the door to see how the dudes were positioned in the living room. Everyone was sitting with their backs to them, watching the fiendishly, amazing Paradice Charms getting fucked on the porno video, *Let Off In Me*.

Doc was the only female in the room and she was sitting front and center. She had nothing on but her thong and bra, looking like something to eat! She had held the dudes off for as long as she could, but the movie was painting all kinds of pictures for them. Lined up against the wall near the front door were four nice sized totes right where Doc said they'd be.

She had come through for Tah once again. It was definitely hard to keep these dudes off of her. They'd been trying to get with her since she started working there six months ago because Doc was bad.

"Come here, Cassey. Help me massage this tension between my legs," the dude that had just left the bathroom said as Phenom slowly moved towards them.

"Nah, I want her to tell me how many licks it's gon' take to get to the center of this Tootsie Roll pop!" the dude to Doc's left said, openly stroking his dick for all to see.

"Why don't I masturbate this desert eagle to the sweet sound of y'all screaming for mercy?" Phenom jumped in, obviously disgusted at how they'd spoke to Doc.

"Huh?" one dude gasped, quickly turning around to see Phenom and Champ standing there.

"What the fuck?" the kid with his dick in his hand replied.

"Nigga? Do you know who shit you're fuck'n wi—," the last kid began, before Phenom helped him find salvation with both of his trigger fingers.

Bok! Bok! Pop! Bok! Pop! Bok! Pop! Pop! BOK!

"About fuck'n time!" Doc spat as she quickly grabbed her clothes and started putting on her blue True Religion jeans, not at all fazed by the scene in front of her. "Another minute and I was undoubtedly about to be raped in this bitch!"

"I don't know. You might've actually like it," Phenom returned, standing there in the thick of gun smoke and debris, lusting over Doc's body as he held his guns at his side.

"Damn!" Champ mumbled, seeing Doc's curves for the first time as felt himself getting an erection.

"Fuck you, Phenom."

"Ummm, can we get the fuck outta here?" Champ asked, trying to keep his eyes off of Doc while trying not to throw up at the same time.

Pulling her blue True Religion shirt over her head as quickly as she could, Doc said, "Yes, lets go."

* * *

An Hour Later

"Sam, where are you? You know we were supposed to be at my mother's house an hour ago," Mrs. Wright informed him over the phone as she sat home in their living room dressed for dinner at her mother's.

"You go ahead. I was just called to a case on the way home," Sergeant Wright replied, racing his red 2008 Ram

1500 Rebel across Bergen Street headed towards Avon Avenue.

"Oh, boy. Why can't Ronnie take this one and fill you in about the details later?"

"Ronnie's at another crime scene over on 9th Avenue. He's the reason they called me to this one."

"I swear this shit is getting so fuck'n old. I might as well be fuck'n single!" she spat, as he drove through Avon Avenue's intersection.

"Don't say that. You make me feel for doing my job."

"Good, cause you also have a job at home taking care of your fuck'n wife that you're doing horrible at, might I add!"

"Trish, I told you that I was going to be spending more time at home once I get this promotion," he replied, preparing to make a right turn up Madison Avenue.

"Whatever, Sam. I'm about to get me a boyfriend on the side or something!"

"Baby, don't talk like that. I promise I'm going to turn my phone off all day tomorrow, so it's just you and me, okay?" he told her, not even realizing she'd already hung up. "Hello? Hello, Trish?"

He looked at his phone and saw the call was over, so he sat his phone on the passenger's seat as he neared 11th Street. He knew he was neglecting his wife in the worse way. But he was he was up for promotion, working hard to get it so he could do more for and with her.

His wife couldn't understand that to get it, he had to put in the time. And some of that time was working on hard cases that were still open. As he turned onto 11th Street, he noticed three figures in dark colored suits, climbing into a black 2013 Volvo S60 with limousine dark tinted windows.

The Volvo S60 pulled off, riding right past Sgt. Wright's 1500 Rebel as he was parking behind the crowd of people that were standing around. He climbed out of the 1500 Rebel and walked over to the crowd, looking past them at the many shell casings. He was definitely at the right place.

While looking for dead bodies, he couldn't get the three suits out of his head or the fact that there were so many shell casings and no bodies. Sgt. Wright walked up to a uniformed officer and flashed his badge. He'd let him know that he was the leading detective on the case.

"What's going on, detective?"

"Another day on the job. What do we have?" Sgt. Wright inquired, pulling out a pack of Newport shorts.

"Two dead inside and one on his way to U.M.D. in critical condition."

"And who were the three spooks that just took off?"

"F.B.I., of course."

Sgt. Wright held his lighter in mid-air with the flame dancing just in front of his cigarette as he replied, "The feds?"

CHAPTER 10
Friday
March 14, 2013
6:45 p.m.

"Daddy, can you start the game for us?" Mya asked, walking into Tah's room with Malani in tow. Both had ketchup and mustard on their faces.

"Yeah, give me a second," Tah repiled as he lifted his head to look in his daughter's direction. He saw both of them standing there looking cute as ever in his t-shirts. Their hair was all wild and their tongues were out in the corners of their mouths, trying to lick off the ketchup and mustard. He burst into laughter and said, "Both of y'all come here."

"What's the matter, daddy? Why come you laughed with us?" Malani asked, as they approached him.

"Not why come. It's how come," he corrected, laughing even harder as both girls walked into his outstretched arms, wrapping their little arms around his neck as he returned a hug. Tah gently kissed both of them on their messy cheeks and said, "And I'm laughing because you two are just too damn cute, and I love y'all."

"We love you, too," Mya replied lovingly.

"Now, can you start us a game for bed?" Malani asked, quickly kissing her father on his right cheek. It was a trick that her and Mya picked up to ensure that they get their way. It was a trick he knew all too well, but each time they did it, it still melted his heart turning him into putty in their hands.

"Yes, I'll start the game for y'all right after y'all go tell grandma to wipe your faces off."

"Okay!" the girls excitedly exclaimed in cheerful unison, before taking off out of the room to find Tammy.

Tah shook his head while still he enjoyed the warm smile that spread across his face. It was nothing like spending time with his girls. Being on house arrest was nothing to him because he was home with his kids but he was still dealing with China being in a coma and Skip still breathing. That was killing him.

Then he had the issue of finding the right lawyer for Phenom. At times, Tah felt the walls were closing in on him when he looked at what was on his shoulders. The only thing that made any sense these days to Tah was Malani, Mya, Travis, Tahiry, and Liz. They were his main focus as of late.

Speaking of Liz, she was on a mission to get pregnant lately. He couldn't understand for the life of him why she wanted a baby so bad by him. They both were very young with two kids and no jobs. Liz did have her own apartment, but it was still a struggle.

Tah was sitting there reading a book titled, *Bad Apple – The Baddest Chick* written by the beautiful, Nisa Santiago. It was the first of an exciting trilogy. Tah stood up and sat the book on on a stack of books Tahiry had bought him. He had asked her to pick him up a bunch of them.

While locked up, Tah had read a few books such as *Cartier Cartel* by Nisa Santiago, *Cruel Execution – Come In Peace Or Leave In Pieces* by Duquie Wilson, *Bad* Blood series by the brother Tuffy, *Animal* series by K'wan, *Thugs Cry* by Cash, and *The Last Of A Dying Breed* by Akbar Prey.

Since Tah read each of those books while he was in the Green Monster, and promised himself he would read a book a day when got home. He walked over to his 32-inch flat screen and turned his Playstation 2 on for the girls, setting up Tetris so that they could just grab the controllers and play when they came back. He sat back down and started thinking about the lick that Phenom and Champ had pulled the other day.

Phenom called to let him know that everything was a go, but Tah was waiting on Champ to bring him the money.

Liz and Tahiry had been out having a drink at Applebee's on Bergen Street and Springfield Avenue. Ever since Tah had been home, Liz had been leaving the girls with their father and hitting the town with Tahiry. Since Tah couldn't move in with her yet, Liz and Mya were staying at Tammy's house at least five days out of the week.

Ever since Phenom and Champ hit that lick the other night on 11th Street, they'd been laying low because of the third victim that was still fighting for his life. Tah told them to until he found what was up from Wheatie. So far everything was clear, but Tah just wanted to make sure.

Tahiry and Liz pulled up in front of Tammy's house both a little tipsy. Liz gave Tahiry a hug and then climbed out of the Lacrosse. She rang the doorbell and Travis came downstairs to let her in. She couldn't just walk in because she didn't have a key. She came in the house with her shopping bags and left overs from Applebee's. Travis was right behind her, closing the door as she proceeded towards Tah's bedroom.

"Girl, Gina said that her landlord is tripping talking about putting her out because of it," Liz told Tabi as she walked into the bedroom with her baby blue Galaxy S3 to her right ear.

"That's so fucked up. I can't believe what Gina is going through," Tabi replied, knowing she was the one that gave Sgt. Wright's source the false information that sent the police to Gina's house.

"I know, right?" Liz expressed. She leaned in and kissed Tah on his lips as he sat on the bed while Mya and Malani played Tetris. "Hey, bae. What you reading?"

"*The Baddest Chick,* part 1," he answered.

"Mommy!" the girls cheered, jumping up to hug Liz as she sat on the bed to Tah's right.

"I take it you're in the house now," Tabi pointed out just as Liz had removed her phone from her ear to hug her and kiss her babies.

"Hey, my babies!" Liz exclaimed overly excited, her arms open for the girls to collapse into her embrace. "I missed y'all so much while I was out with Auntie Tahi and Auntie Stacie! Was y'all good for daddy and gandma Tammy while mommy was gone?"

"Daddy prayed kitchen wit' us and did dress up," Malani excitedly confessed, climbing up onto Liz's lap opposite Mya who had already claimed Liz' right leg.

"Oh, he did, did he?"

"Uh huh. And, and, and he played color books with us, too," Mya replied, while Liz leaned over and gave Tah another kiss on his lips.

"Wow," Liz gasped, smiling endlessly because her girls had a great father in their lives. "You guys are lucky to have a dad that does great things with you, right?"

"Yeah!" both girls cheered in unison.

"Not lucky, but blessed," Tah said as his 2S began to vibrate. "We're Muslim. We don't believe in luck. We are blessed through the mercy and grace of Allah."

"Who is that?" Liz questioned as Tah looked at his phone to see who was texting him.

"None ya!"

"Don't play with me, Tahiem."

Champ: The food is ready. You want me to bring it to you now?

"I'm not playing. It's none ya texting me," he said, laughed while he texted Champ back.

"Excuse me, girls.Mmommy needs to put hands on with daddy real quick 'cause he thinks that I'm playing with him," Liz said, letting the girls down off of her lap. "Tah, who the fuck are you texting?"

"Oooh, mommy cursing!" the girls teased, pointing their little index fingers at Liz.

"I know," Tah replied, turning to face an upset Liz. "And she better watch her mouth in front of y'all."

"I'm sorry, girls. Y'all go ahead and tell grandma to run y'all a bath so I can put y'all to bed," Liz instructed them before focusing back on Tah. "Tahiem Muhammad, who are you texting?"

"None ya damn business!" he replied jokingly as the girls stood there smiling. He had pressed the send button just before Liz aggressively snatched the phone out of his hands.

Tah: Nah, bring it to me in the morning. My baby cooked already.

"Oooohh, you lucky," Liz snapped, after finding out he was texting Champ and not some chick. "Stop playing with me, Tahiem. I will hurt a bitch over mine!"

"Awwww, you look so cute when you get jealous," he said, grabbing her chin and lightly squeezing it, whle Liz sat his phone on the bed between them.

"Don't touch me! you play too damn much!" she said, swatting his hand away from her chin.

"You sure you don't me touching you?" Tah asked, wrapping his arms around her and pulling her into a bear hug.

"Stop. Get off of me," Liz smiled, pulling away from him. She then stood up and ran towards the door and said, "Come on, girls. It's time to take y'all bath so y'all can get ready for bed."

"Do we have to?" Mya whined, running over to her father and wrapping her arms around his right leg.

"Yes, you have to. Now let's go, both of y'all," she said as Malani followed her sister and grabbed Tah's left leg, both giving him the puppy dog eyes.

"Daddy, we not tired," Mya whined.

"I said lets go. Mommy and daddy wanna spend some alone time together."

"Y'all go ahead and take y'all baths, then go lay with grandma and watch TV until you fall asleep," Tah told them, knowing they weren't going to budge if he didn't say something.

"So we not have to go bed?" Malani asked, laying her little head on Tah's knee.

"Yes, y'all are going to be—"

"No, y'all can go in the room with grandma and watch TV, but if y'all don't be good, then I'm putting y'all to bed."

"We gon' be good," the girls yelled excitedly, running out of the room.

"I can't stand yo' ass!" Liz said, looking at him with squinted eyes, feeling like his was taking control of her girls. "You got that for now but wait until mommy gets her power back."

"Whatever. Go bathe the kids and bring your ass back so I can do some things to that pussy!" he replied.

"Just nasty," Liz said, blushing.

She pulled her earrings out of her ears and laid them on top of Tah's nightstand, then slid out of her light blue Seven jeans. She didn't have far to walk to put her clothes in the dirty clothes hamper because the closet was right there just a few feet away from the bed. The room had become even more over crowded now that Liz and Mya was there.

Tah picked his book back up and began reading again as Liz walked the girls out of the room in her white G-string and t-shirt, causing him to watch as her ass cheeks bounced sexily with each step. His dick instantly became erect just from looking at her. He couldn't deny the had a beautiful woman and even though he lusted over other women, he had the total package with Elizabeth Kimbrough.

* * *

2:47 p.m. The Next Day

"Did you talk to Champ yet?" Doug asked Doc as they sat in Tahiry's Lacrosse which was parked on the corner behind building 100.

"Nah, he hasn't answered any of my calls since we dumped his ass at the hospital the other night," Doc replied, bobbing her head to Nas' "One Mic" as it leaked out of the speakers.

"Well, is the nigga alive at least?"

"Yeah, Tah said he texted him the next day. You know how these niggas be in their feelings and shit worse than bitches!"

"Hell yeah."

"Doug, pass me those two ditches from between the seat!" Tabi yelled from the gate where she was sitting in her beach chair.

"Damn, didn't y'all hoes just smoke a blunt?" Vee asked, while serving a fiend three bags of dope.

"I'm telling you," Jerm joined in, snaking his neck sassily.

"Didn't you just drink a Bud Ice?" Liz asked, passing Tabi a bag of sour diesel.

"Bitch, don't worry about how many beers I drink. I don't drink nearly as much as y'all smoke!" Vee snapped, taking a gulp of her 24-ounce can of Bud Ice.

"Here, Tab!" Doug called out, holding the two vanilla Dutch masters out of the window in her right hand.

"Where the fuck is Tahiry?" Doc questioned, looking towards the building.

"Ladies, ladies," GK greeted, walking up on them with two of his little homies in tow.

"GK, what's good?" Tabi returned, while grabbing the cigars from Doug.

"I can't call it. Liz, let me holla at you real quick."

"What's up?" Liz asked, standing up and walking towards him.

"Here, this is another six stacks to go towards the home girl's medical bills," GK answered, handing Liz the money while looking her up and down. "Still no word on the nigga Skip?"

"Tah said that he got it handled and y'all can chill out. He said Skip gon' be meeting his brothers real soon," she replied, smiling at that fact that her man was handling business as he promised.

"A'ight, tell son that I appreciate everything that he's done for China. That's real nigga shit, and if he needs anything to just let me know."

"I sure will."

"How's China holding up?"

"GK, stop staring at me like that, nigga! You like my big brother!" Liz spat, feeling uncomfortable with the way he was staring at her titties.

"My bad. You getting thick, girl. You better tell Tah to keep a leash on you. Niggas be checking for you."

"Whatever, the only nigga that can touch this is Tahiem Muhammad! Know that!" Liz spat, letting it be known who she belonged to.

"Lucky him!" GK returned, licking his lips seductively.

"Whatever. We just came from seeing China. She's still the same, so I guess that's a good thing since she hasn't gotten any worse," she informed him, while stuffing the money into her green Michael Kors handbag.

"Trillz, that's what's up. Look, you go ahead and put that money up before something happens to it," GK said as a cherry top police car drove up Madison.

"Yeah, you right."

"Later, beautiful."

"A'ight, GK," Liz said as they embraced in a hug as Tahiry was coming out of the building carrying a black Nike book bag.

Two fiends walked up to the building with a Pathmark shopping cart full of crushed cans and steel pipes. They walked right up to Jerm and Vee. Jerm stood near the back door of building 100 in a pair of skin tight white JCME jeggings, a pink True Religion t-shirt, and a pair of pink Nike ACG boots. Though Jerm was a homosexual and was blatantly flamboyant with his sexual preference, he knew he was a man and not a woman.

Jerm would ride for his homegirls in the blink of an eye. He just so happened to be more attracted to men instead of women. Tah, Champ, and Phenom never judged him because they knew what he was into before he was confident enough to admit it to himself.

Tah fought many dudes that tried to clown or attack Jerm because of who he was. Jerm didn't have AIDS nor was he contagious. Now Tah wasn't into the whole homosexual thing. However, him and Jerm grew up together since they were little kids and he loved him like a brother. The crew let it be known that Jerm was one of them and if you fucked with him, you had to fuck with all of them.

Jerm and Vee were the ones that put the most work in on the block. They really did the hand-to-hand part while Doug and Tabi collected the money. Doc and Liz usually did the packaging since Mona, Lissa, and Chela were locked up, while Tahiry did the negotiating for them.

GK broke their embrace and turned to leave as he savored the lingering scent of Liz's Paris Hilton CanCan perfume, heading back towards Clinton Avenue. GK knew Liz was a rare breed. He had made several moves trying to get at her, but Liz was dead lock faithful to her man. Every time that GK or any other dude did, she'd tell Tah immediately. That made him respect and love her that much more.

As GK walked off with his little homies, they all took in Liz's appearance as she stood there in her brown Hermes halter mini dress that had an exposing and enticing neckline that showed off her succulent cleavage. On her feet was a pair of green and brown Hermes soft bottom sneakers. This outfit cost her all of the money she had saved up.

Her hair was done up in blonde Marley twist which were dark brown at the root, pulled into a ponytail so she could show off her new tattoo. She had a tattoo of a skeleton plat formed heart with Tah's name sketched through it. She had gotten it earlier today.

Before the little homies turned around completely, they got a full view of Liz's ass in that dress, jiggling freely with thunderous conviction. She walked in full stride towards Tahiry who was looking good in her tight fitted blue True Religion jeans, orange True Religion tank top, and a pair of blue and orange Nike Air Maxs, getting her thug on.

Liz walked up to Tahiry just as she was approached the trunk of her Lacrosse, gripping the book bag that Phenom had dropped off that extra tight in her left hand.

In her right hand was her S2 that was open to her text screen. She was texing back and forth with Tah. He was home waiting for her to drop his money off. Liz stood off to the side watching Tahiry's every move. She was trying to figure out what her bestfriend was doing. Tahiry opened her trunk and quickly tossed the book bag inside, then leaned to, grab her baby glock .22 that Tah gave her.

Liz wanted to ask Tahiry so badly what the hell was in the book bag and what did she and Tah have to talk about so much lately, but she knew Tahiry. She wasn't going to tell her a damn thing.

True, they were bestfriends and they told one another everything, but at the end of the day, Tahiry's loyalty did and would forever remain with Tah. Tahiry stuffed her .22 inside of her black Juicy Couture bag as she closed the trunk, stepping towards the sidewalk next to Liz.

"Come on, Beth. Your man told me to bring your ass home," Tahiry informed, smiling warmly.

"I know his ass don't want nothing. Probably getting tired of Malani and Mya begging him to play doll babies with them," Liz said and laughed as she reached for the passenger door handle.

"I don't know. He just asked me to bring your ass up the street."

* * *

Minutes Later Up the Street

"Allahu Akbar Allahu Akbar, Ash-Hadu An La Ilaha Ill-Allah, Ash-Hadu Anna Muhammadan Rasul-Ullah, Haiya Ala Salat, Haiya Falat, Qumat Is Salat Qumat Is Salat, Allah Akbar Allah Akbar, La Ilaha Ill-Allah." Phenom chanted beautifully, standing atop his musalla.

Phenom stood behind Tah as he was up front standing on his musalla, leading them into Maghrib salat. Travis stood to Phenom's left and Champ stood to his right. The four of them had just finished purifying themselves by performing Wudu.

They each proudly wore their Islamic garbs and their kufis on top their heads.

"Subhanaka Allahumma Wa Bihamdika Wa Tabaraka Ismuka Wa Ta A'ala Jadduka Wa La Ilaha Ghayruk ," Tah firmly said, reciting the Du'aa-ul-istiftaah. That meant praise and glory is to Allah. Blessed is your name and exalted is your majesty and glory. There is no true God but you.

Tah continued by chanting, "A'udhu Billahi Min Ash-shaytanir-rajim ,Bismillahir Rahmanir Raheem, Alhamdu Lillahi Rabbil Alameen, Ar Rahmanir." That meant I seek the protection of Allah against the accused Satan.

As Tah began the Al-fatihah, Tahiry and Liz were downstairs getting out of Tahiry's Lacrosse, causing heads to turn in their direction. It only took Tahiry maybe four minutes to drive up the street to Tammy's house from Chadwick Avenue. Being that close to the hood was always a plus for Tah.

Tahiry grabbed the book bag out of the trunk and proceeded towards the porch with Liz right behind her. There were several Bloods standing on the corner watching and lusting over the two of them, but they all knew who they were. When they reached the second floor, Liz went to knock but Tahiry stopped her and pulled out her keys. She stuck them into the keyhole and twisted the knob.

Tahiry had had a key to since Tammy moved into the apartment, but Liz never really paid it any attention until now. Once again, Tahiry was Liz's girl but in her mind, she was getting tired of Tahiry and Tah's quote/ unquote brother/sister relationship. She was a woman at the end of the day and seeing another woman so close to her man was getting to her.

"Tahi, I didn't know that you had a key," Liz said to her as the two of them walked into the apartment.

"Girl, bye. I've had this key since they first moved in. Tah ain't give you a key yet?"

"Yeah, right!"

"As much as you stay here and as lazy as everybody in here is, I'm shocked that you don't have one," she returned, turning around to lock the door back as Liz continued towards Tah's bedroom.

Liz stormed into Tah's room ready to lash out but he wasn't there. She looked over at the cable box and saw the time, knowing now where he was. She had been with Tah long enough to know what times of the day that he offered salat.

She was so aware of the prayer schedule, she would call him to make sure he was preparing to offer salat. That was just another reason why Tah loved the ground that Liz walked on. The next thing she noticed were a bunch of newspapers spread out across the bed accompanied by a book titled *Crime Pays* by Tha Twinz.

She had no idea why he had all of those newspapers on the bed like that, but once he finished offering salat, she was damn sure going to find out. Tahiry walked into the room and sat the book bag behind the door and then looked at the bed. She too was shocked at the way his bed looked.

In all of the years she'd been around Tah, she knew him to be a neat freak. This wasn't like him, but she knew that he had to have had a good reason why his bed was this way. Tahiry gave Liz a hug and kissed her right cheek before spinning on her heels and leaving out of the room, while Liz looked for answers. No sooner than Tahiry left, Champ and Travis came walking out of the closet with their musallas in their hands.

"As salaamu alaikum, sis," Travis greeted, walking past her and heading straight out of the room without waiting for a response.

"Wa alaikum as salaam," Liz replied, giving the proper greeting back as Tah had taught her.

"As salaamu alaikum, Liz," Champ greeted as he walked over to the bed and grabbed his iPhone, walking out of the room following Travis.

"Wa alaikum as salaam."

"As salaamu alaikum, bruh," Phenom greeted lowly as him and Tah came strolling out of the closet.

"Wa alaikum as salaam wa rahmatullah," Tah returned as Phenom gave Liz a hug and a kiss on her forehead.

"Hey, Greg."

"Make sure you call my phone and let me know what's what," Tah told Phenom.

"I got you, skoob," Phenom told him, releasing Liz.

"Nough said make sure you lock the door on the way out."

"Bye, Greg."

"Never bye, but always see you later. You say bye to a person that's dead," Phenom replied, before leaving the room.

As soon as Phenom walked out of the room, Liz turned towards Tah and said, "Tahiem, there are some things we need to discuss and I need you to keep it real funky with me."

"You know what, you're right. There are some massive things that you and I need to talk about. However, let's start looking for a house in the meantime in between time," Tah replied, patting the spot on his bed to his right where he wanted her to sit.

"Hold, hold on," Liz stuttered, closing her eyes and then opening them wider than they were before she closed them. "Boy, did you just say let's look for a house?"

"I mean we could always just stay on Chadwick in your apartment, or better yet, we could just stay right in here with Tammy," he said, smiling.

"Tah, don't fuck'n play with me like this. You wanna look for a house!" Liz exclaimed excitedly, forgetting everything she was about to snap on him about.

Picking up a piece of the newspaper that was the Classified section, Tah simply replied, "Yes, a house."

"Oh my fuck'n God! I love you so much! I swear to God, I love you so much!" she screamed excitedly, jumping into his arms, nearly knocking him over.

"I love you, too."

"A house for just you and I?"

"No, a house for you, me, Malani, Mya, and Travis."

"Oh, my God! I love you!" Liz confessed with tears in her eyes as she leaned in and gave him a sloppy but very passionate kiss. Then she pulled away and said, "I love you, I love you, I love you! Oh my God! I fuck'n love your black ass sooooo much!"

"I love you, too," Tah replied, grabbing Liz so she could sit still long enough to look her in her eyes. "Will you move with me?"

At that moment in time, everything seemed to come to a nail-pounding standstill from her, her heart rate quickly skyrocketing to a extreme rapid speed. Her mouth fell open with no remembrance of sound. Her palms became possessed with sweat, and her knees weakened as her head took on the weight of a feather as light as it was.

Her throat quickly turned into a replica of a desert it was so dry. The Nile River couldn't compare to the flow of tears running down her cheeks. There was so much emotion coming out of her right then. Never in a million years did she ever think that Tah would come around and become her boyfriend let alone buy her a house!

Sitting there on Tah's lap somewhat shell shocked and nervous, all Liz could muster up was, "Bae, what did you do?"

"Huh?"

"What did you do, Tahiem? What did you do?" Liz asked, beginning to tremble uncontrollably.

"What did I do?"

"Don't play stupid, Tah. What did you do made you all of a sudden wanna move with me? Just days ago you wasn't sure if you even wanted to commit to me and move together and now you wanna buy me a house? What did you do? Tell me!"

"What did I do?"

"Yes, nigga! What the fuck did you do!"

Wiping the tears from her face as he tried to not to ruin her MAC makeup, he kissed her softly on her lips as he looked into her soul. He told her, "I fell in love."

Liz felt like she was being reborn all over again, and even though Tah didn't come bearing a huge engagement ring, the way he'd just confessed his love for her was more than any ring he could've gotten her. It was priceless.

Liz pressed her lips against his as if they were the key to heaven. She knew she could keep her lips like that forever. She leaned forward forcing Tah's body back so he laying flat on the bed. She got on top of him, kissing him like she'd never kissed him before. He had both of his hands gripping her soft 42-inch ass, while helping her dress rise to the occasion as his dick became rock hard pressing against her stomach through the blue Levi jeans.

Liz straddled Tah after sliding her size 3 feet out of her Hermes sneakers, positioning herself on top of his erection. Tah slid hands over her now exposed ass, pulling her G-string from between her ass cheeks. He gently slid his right index and middle fingers into Liz's drowning, wet pussy.

After Tah took his fingers out of her pussy, he slid them into his mouth sucking her juices off. She kissed him deeply just to taste herself and said, "Yes, yes, baby! I will move with you!"

CHAPTER 11
Friday
March 14, 2014
6:10 p.m.

"There are two factors that influence the degree of difficulty in patience. First is the degree of motivation when man wants to do something. The secondlyis how convenient is the intended action for man. If both factors exist, patience reaches it utmost difficulty and vice versa. If one of the two factors disappear, it becomes difficult on one hand and considerably convenient on the other," the Iman delivered as he stood before his community draped in his Muslim garbs.

Thus, if man has no motive to kill, steal, drink wine, or commit atrocities, and these actions are inconvenient for him, then he is able to ward them off easily. Whereas a man whose desires are powerful and finds it convenient to act accordingly, then he's hardly able to show constant perseverance. Hence, the ruler who abstains from injustice, the young man from indecency and the rich from worldly pleasures, command the highest status before, Allah.

These categories rightly deserve, Allah's protection on the Day of Judgment so long as they bear hardships patiently. Therefore, the adulterous old man, the untruthful ruler, and the haughty poor are severely punished because it would be more convenient for them to overcome such unlawful desires. Consequently, giving up patience in such situations sheds light on their insolence and rebellion."

Tah sat three rows back with Champ to his left and Phenom to his right. They were attending Islamic studies or Talim, which was the only thing that Tah was able to leave the house for other than Jumah. They were down on High Street also known as Dr. Martin Luther King Jr. Boulevard and W.

Kinney Street at Rahman's Masjid. It was right next to Prince's Chicken Shack.

It used to be Utah's Chicken Shack back in the day, a chicken shack where you could get your head blown off while waiting on your order. The new Hill Manor was now up and people were residing there. The new Brick Towers was nearly complete.

The community was slowly getting back to the way it was before the city of Newark knocked down all of the buildings where they started with the Prince Street projects back in 2001. Tah was happy to be out of the house, but he was even more happy to be amongst his brothers and sisters of Islam. There was nothing that he cherished more than Allah.

Every time he came to Rahman's, he learned something that he took with him in life. With the life he was him living, he was living he needed Allah and his mercy. Tah was all ears as the Iman spoke about because patience that was something he was dealing with daily. With everything that he had on his plate, patience was highly needed.

Champ sat there with his arm in a sling after taking a bullet to the arm the night of the lick. Shit had gotten real when they left out of the workhouse. The dudes from across the street had noticed Doug sitting in front of the workhouse too long, so they went and grabbed their guns to investigate. That's when Doc, Phenom, and Champ came out of the workhouse.

The three of them were each carrying a tote, looking around suspiciously. That's when the shots started ringing out. Phenom dropped his tote and returned fire, while Doc and Champ loaded the totes into the Regal. Doug sat in the driver's seat also returning fire.

This backed the dudes up, giving the crew the time they needed to get in the car and make a getaway. But as soon as Doug pulled off, a bullet entered the car and tore right into

Champ's left elbow. He was pissed about getting shot and had been distant ever since it happened.

He really blamed Tah because he felt he knew he should have never been there in the first place. However, Champ wasn't about to cry over spilled milk. What was done was done and there was nothing either of them could do about it. He was alive. That's all that mattered in the end.

"On the authority of Abu Hurairah, the Prophet, peace be upon him says, Seven are those whom Allah will place under his protection on a day when there will be no protection but his name. The just ruler, the young man who is brought up in worship of his Lord, a man whose heart is constantly attached to Mosques. Two men who love one another for Allah's sake. He alone brings them together and separates them. A man who, summoned by a beautiful woman says, I fear, Allah. A man who gives charity so secretly that his left hand does not know not what his right hand has given, and a man, who remembering Allah in seclusion, then sheds tears against Allah," the Iman continued as he read from the book "The Way To Patience And Gratitude".

It requires constant perseverance to keep away from sins of the tongue and unchastely because their motives are powerful and easily accessible. Unfortunately, sins of the tongue provide delight for man, such as slander, telling lies, dispute, direct or indirect self-complacency, reporting people's utterances, deframing enemies, and praising his votaries. On the authority of Mu'adh Ibn Jabal, may Allah be pleased with him that the Prophet,peace be upon him, said—"

Tah was amazed at what he was hearing. He loved to learn new things about the faith of Islam. He wanted to know as much about who he was as possible. Champ sat there nodding his head up and down with a huge smile plastered across his

113

face. He too was learning new things about Islam that he didn't know.

He was extremely intelligent but when it came to Islam, he was still learning the basics. This was something that could keep his mind going until the death. Phenom was deeply pulled in because of the things he was doing out in the streets. He needed Allah with him everywhere he went and he didn't miss a salat. He had many sins he needed to constantly wipe out. He knew that Allah. See, everything that he was doing was out there in the streets.

The wrath of Allah was the only thing he feared as he did evil shit from time to time. Allah's, mercy was the only thing he was concerned with. Tah knew all about Phenom's upbringing, so and he understood how Phenom felt when it came to murder. It was a sense of art for Phenom, his stress reliever. For the three young men sitting there listening, they felt like each word was directed at them in one way or another. Even the brother Tarin was in attendance, sucking in as much as he could.

The Iman continued reading from "The Way To Patience And Gratitude", stopping in between to explain certain things to the brothers. The Iman read and explained until it was time to offer Maghrib as the brothers came together and offered salat as a community. Once salat was finished, the brothers started leaving out of the Masjid exchanging greetings and handshakes. Tah walked beside Tarin telling him about his latest troubles.

Tarin was dressed in a pair of dark blue JCME boot cut jeans, a black True Religion long sleeve t-shirt, a black Newark Brick City fitted, and a pair of black JCME Vasquez boots that resembled Gore Tex boots. He too was going through some legal problems that he was fighting.

Tah wasn't alone in that category. The police knew how to come down on those trying to make a living for themselves and their family. He was enjoying his night on the streets truly missing his freedom. Champ had jumped into a cab and left. He had to pack so he could get ready to go down to Millville. He needed to make sure that he didn't forget anything.

Phenom, on the other hand, was right behind Tah and Tarin. He was walking a foot behind them with his desert eagle in the waistline of his blue True Religion jeans covered by his white North Face thermal. The three of them walked towards Tarin's dark brown Oldsmobile Bonneville. Behind his Bonneville was his little homies sitting inside of his rusted, blood red Chevrolet Suburban with dark red limousine tinted windows.

Tah and Tarin became close after spending a lot of time at the Masjid together over the years. Plus, Tarin knew Mujid and respected his gangster. He'd known Tah for years, but they were into two different things. Now Islam had brought them together in a positive way, bringing a group of brothers together instead of separating them.

"Man, I got mad shit going on right now. I got this dumbass case over my head which I'm on house arrest for," Tah began, looking over at Tarin. "Then I gotta handle this other situation with Phenom."

"What situation?" Tarin asked, giving him a quizzed facial expression.

"He might have a case. I'm tryin' to get him a lawyer, but the one I got is a waste of time."

"Look, give me your number. I'm gon' holla at me peoples and have him get in touch with you."

"Nah, it ain't that type of party. This case is grade A serious. We're talking life sentence seriously," he informed him, trying to explain that Phenom was looking at murder charges.

"Listen, he got my man Dope out of a life sentence after he was already sentenced to life without parole. When I tell you he's good, I mean just that!" Tarin replied as two of his homies climbed out of the Suburban with guns in their hands.

"A'ight, what are his prices like?"

"He's expensive ,but I'm gon' tell him to give you the best deal he can without cheating himself. I got love for y'all. Plus, I can't drain my brothers for a cause that's for the better."

"That's what's up. My number is eight, six two, five, five five, three, six, three seven., Have him call me and I'll get him that money as soon as he can meet up with me." Tah said, as Tarin climbed into his Bonneville sticking the key into the ignition.

"Trillz, I'ma do that as soon as I turn my phone back on, you said eight, six two, five, five five, three, six, three seven , right?"

"Yeah, good looking, Okhi."

"It ain't about nothing. As salaamu alaikum wa rahmatullah."

"Wa alaikum as salaam wa rahmatullah wa barrakatu," both Tah and Phenom returned, standing there feeling like they had just accomplished something.

Tarin pulled away from the curb, the Suburban filled with his little homies right behind him. Tah turned to Phenom and said, "I'ma handle this while you make that move. Make sure you hit my phone as soon as you touch down. I'm gon' have Doc and Tabi bring that to you."

"A'ight, I got you."

* * *

Monday
May 19, 2014
9:24 p.m. Trenton. New Jersey

"Damn, it's mad bitches out tonight," Bino said, as Rah was parking.

Only thing certain is death
When I squeeze ten
I'ma watch all of them jerk in his chest
They wanna talk about peace
I'ma piss in the dirt/ spit on the flowers fuck if he rest
I'ma show you what a animal is
Cut his hands off
Cause I ain't like the way he handled his biz
I get a lot more violenter
I swear to, God, and like
What I wouldn't do for a shotgun silencer

"Yo, that's my shit right there, nef! A bitch could listen to that all day and never get tired of it," Rah confessed as he climbed out of his midnight red Chevrolet Equinox, adjusting the black P-89 ruger on his waist.

"I see!" Bino returned, looking up and down Olden Avenue and East State Street. "All a bitch listen to is D-Block from sun up to sun down, nef."

"Yeah, a'ight, nigga." Rah laughed, noticing a short light skin chick squinting her eyes in their direction.

"Bino, is that you?" she asked.

"Yo, who the fuck is that?"

"I don't know, mu'fucka!" Bino replied, looking at the girl with a confused look on his face.

"Bino, why you ain't call me yet?" the girl asked, standing in front of the chicken shack with three other females.

"'Cause a bitch don't want your stalking ass following them around the town all day!" the chick standing to her left in a yellow minidress shot back before Bino could reply.

"Damn, nigga! A bitch ain't tell me you had bitches like this on standby!" Rah said as they approached the entrance of the chicken shack.

"Shit, nigga. I forgot all about her. You know Shay be going through my phone and shit," Bino said, loud enough for her to hear him. "She probably deleted her number out of my phone."

"Oooh, you let the wife find my number and erase it?" she said, shaking head from left to right disappointment, as Rah walked up on the girl with the minidress on.

"What's poppin', shorty? What's your name?" Rah questioned, tossing his right arm around her shoulders, leading her into the chicken shack.

"I'm Lemur and this is my sister, Leopard," Lee replied, stopping to turning around to face the other three girls. When she did, a white Jeep Cherokee pulled up in front of the chicken shack playing Tupac's "Keep Ya Head Up". "And that's my other sister, Lemming, and her two friends, KeKe and Lisa."

And I remember Marvin Gaye use to sing to me
He had me feeling like black was the thing to be
And suddenly the ghetto didn't seem so tough
And though we had it rough was always had enough
I often fussed about my curfew and broke the rules
Ran with the local crew and had a smoke or two

"Damn, that's right. Your name is Leo. We met at the big ass cookout at Columbus Park the other week," Bino said, wrapping his left arm around her shoulder, escorting her towards the chicken shack. "I did mean to hit you up, but a bitch be so busy chasing this paper and beating down the studio."

"That's alright. I'm just glad that you ain't forget about me, that's all." Leo smiled, trying as hard as she could not to blush at the way Bino was looking at her.

"Nah, never that," he told her as they all stepped into the chicken shack where ten people were already standing after placing their order. "You want something?"

"Yeah," she replied, smiling harder than ever because she was seen with Bino by a crowd of people from the hood.

"Bino? What's up, brother?" the young Arabian kid, Rabsaj, greeted him from behind the counter. "What can I get you, my brother?"

"Saj, let me get two Italian cheeseburgers, an orange Vitamin Water, a fruit punch Cand C, three vanilla dutches, and a pack of Newport one hundreds," Rah jumped in before Bino could respond. "And a fifty-cent Bic lighter."

"What you want, Leo?" Bino asked before telling Rabsaj what he wanted as he wrote down Rah's order.

"Umm, what can I get?" Leo asked, looking at the menu that was on the wall.

"Get whatever you want," he told her, pulling out a gas station size wad of twenties, fifties, and one hundred dollar bills from his right front pocket.

"Okay, I want a breast, two legs, and a biscuit," Leo answered, not trying to be greedy.

"You don't want nothing to drink?" Rabsaj asked her, writing down her order.

"Go ahead," Bino said as she looked to him for confirmation.

"A lemonade Vitamin Water."

"We don't got no more lemonade Vitamin Waters," Rabsaj informed her.

"Okay, let me get a XXX Vitamin Water then."

"Okay. What can I get you, Bino?"

"Give me a half and half Gold Peak tea, ten vanilla dutches, and a pack of Black and Milds," Bino told him, peeling three twenty dollar bills off of his stack and sitting it on the counter. "Ring Rah's order up with mine. I'm paying for both of them."

"Got damn. How many blunts is y'all goin' smoke?" KeKe gasped, standing behind Rah and Lee as the young hustlers in the chicken shack gawked at Lee and Leo because they were with them.

"Don't worry about it. Y'all ain't goin' be partying with us any way, with y'all lil' asses!" Lee snapped, already claiming Rah before he could claim her.

"Rob Bino? Nigga, is that you?"

Hearing that specific name called out, Bino turned around. He saw the person behind the voice even though he already knew who it was before he did. "Mu'fuck'n, Dez. What's really fuck'n good, nef!"

"I thought that was your ass over there standing in the front of the jawn stunting with all of that money out like a bull won't rob your ass," Dez replied. As he walked up, they slapped palms before embracing one another in a brotherly hug.

"Nah, that ain't goin' happen to a bitch around here," he returned, breaking their embrace as Leo stepped next to him claiming her position.

"I heard that."

"Damn, nef. What you doing out in a bitch neck of the woods?"

"I been fuck'n with this lil' chick that lives off of Greenwood. She held the bull down throughout my last stretch," Dez admitted.

"Oh, a'ight. So you just coming home then?"

"Nah, I been home now for like four months. I just been laying low trying to catch a bull slipping. You know how I get down already with these jawns," Dez said, tapping the chrome .357 magnum tucked in the waistline of his blue True Religion jeans that was concealed under his black Polo shirt.

"Say no more," Bino said, looking past him at the kid standing behind him.

"What's up with nef ? He with you?"

"Yeah, this baby girl's lil' brother. The young bull is harmless."

"If you say so. But anyway, this my man, Rah. The goofy nigga I was telling you about down the way," he told him as Rah stood off to the side analyzing Dez and the situation at hand. "Rah, this my man, Dez. This the nigga I was telling you about when a bitch was down the Ville." The Ville was the Garden State Youth Correctional Facility.

The whole group walked out of the chicken shack with their food in hand, each one in their own conversation as Bino's phone started to vibrate. He looked down at the screen to make sure that Shay wasn't calling him while he was all hugged up with Leo.

Seeing that it was Young, he quickly answered the call. "What's good, nef?"

"Aye, there's some nigga around here from Newark talking about a bitch family and shit," Young replied through the phone, standing on the block.

"A'ight, let him know I'm on my way right now."

"A'ight."

"What's the word, nef?" Rah questioned, looking at Bino as he slid his phone back in his pocket. He knew what they were waiting on.

"It's on, nef. Cuz just got down here," Bino excitedly replied, turning towards Dez. "Dez, take this ride with me real quick."

"Let's ride," he said without thinking twice as he gave Bino a wicked grin.

"Leo, I'ma call you later, a'ight?" Bino told her with his right arm wrapped around her thin waist.

"Umm hmm, like you did last time," she replied lowly with much disappointment.

"Here, put your number in my phone again. I'ma hit you in like a hour on everything," he said, pulling his phone back out and handing it to her.

Leo quickly grabbed his phone and stored her number in it, but this time she didn't half step. She text her phone from his phone so if he didn't call, then she could call him.

"I got you," Leo said, handing Bino his phone back. Mario's "Let Me Love You" ringtone confirmed she had received the text.

"A'ight, give me about an hour."

"I'll be waiting."

"I'm seeing you later, Rah?" Lee nervously asked.

"Yeah, I'ma come snatch your lil' ass up when I'm done," Rah said, already on his way towards the Equinox.

Around the corner on Walnut Street and South Walter Avenue, Phenom sat inside of the same Regal they used for the robbery. He was going through his phone looking at the pictures of Stacie while waiting on Bino. On the passenger seat was the dark red blood stain from where Champ bled after he got shot. Because the car was tucked away, he didn't get it cleaned out. Since the interior was a dark blue color, it was kind of hard to see but one could definitely see something was there.

In the backseat sat a black Northface book bag with five bricks of dope and twenty grams of raw. Doc had just left with Tabi after driving the drugs down for Tah to give to Phenom. Tah had come off with the mother load and was sitting nicely right now. So he had to hurry up and put his plan into motion.

They taken thirty kilos of raw cocaine, fifteen kilos of raw uncut dope, and twenty-five pounds of grade A haze weed, and forty bags of ecstasy pills which contained 100,000 in each bag. In the back room of the workhouse, Phenom had found $75,000 in the closet stuffed in three shoeboxes.

Tah had read *B.M.F. – The Rise And Fall Of Big Meech And The Black Mafia Family* written by Mara Shalhop. When reading it, he saw what greatness was supposed to be like. He knew he wasn't Demetrius "Big Meech" Flenory or Terry "Southwest" Flenory. Still, he couldn't deny that the brothers inspired him.

Tah and Phenom wanted to be the next Wayne and Mad Max off he movie *Shottas*, and Bumpy Johnson and Frank Lucas of Harlem, New York. The only difference was Tah had plans on getting his and getting as low as he could before the life drowned him, while Phenom was content with dying in the life. Phenom planned to make as much money as he could until he was either dead or in jail with football numbers. He knew exactly what he wanted out of the streets and what to look forward to getting in the end.

Phenom was Bino's first cousin on his father's side. They met when Bino when he was up in Yonkers, New York visiting his grandmother one summer. They exchanged numbers when they learned they were both from Jersey.

Phenom had visited Trenton a few times before today, even hooking up with a few chicks in the process. So, it was a no-brainer where Phenom had decided to run to Trenton after Tah told him to get low until he got him a lawyer. Tah was looking for the very best. Phenom didn't have Bino's new number, so he pulled up on the block he knew Bino hustled on, trying to catch him. Instead, he ran into Young who called him for him.

Phenom had spoken to Bino earlier on his house phone, so he knew he was coming down and why. When Phenom called the house phone back, Shay told him that Bino there. Just as he was starting to get restless Bino pulled up in the Equinox and double parked next to the Regal, boxing Phenom in.

Bino, Rah, Dez, and Dez's girlfriend's little brother all climbed out of the Equinox. They rushed across the street not realizing he was still in the car. Phenom grabbed the book bag and climbed out of the Regal once he seen Bino hop out of the Equinox. Bino turned around when Young pointed in Phenom's direction. He had the biggest smile on his face as he walked towards his cousin.

Though Bino was 30 years old, he still looked like he was every bit of 26. Jail kept him stuck in his youth over the years. As Bino extended his right hand to greet Phenom, he noticed the scowl on his cousin's face. Phenom knew Rah from his past visits to Trenton, but he didn't know Dez or the kid that he was with. It didn't take long for everyone to notice Phenom's discomfort.

"Yo, son. What the fuck is this shit?" Phenom barked, pointing behind Bino.

"Cool out, nef. These my niggas. You know that I don't roll like that," Bino shot back, feeling offended.

"This fuck'n nigga looks like a got damn cop!" he barked, pointing at the young kid before turning towards Dez. "And this pretty boy as nigga looks like a fuck'n undercover!"

As a white Audi A4 drove by with Ghostface's "Back Like That" pumping out of the speakers, Dez squinted his eyes slowly nodding his head.

He reached into his waistline and yanked his .357, causing Phenom to drop the book bag and draw his desert eagle. The two dudes that thought so much alike. Before anybody knew what was happening, Dez spun on his heels to his left, pressing the barrel to his girlfriend's brother's right temple.

Doom! Doom! Doom!

"Oh shit!" Young screeched as blood and brain matter splashed all over his face.

"Yo, Bino! What the fuck, nef!" one of the young hustlers a few houses down snapped as the kid's body hit the pavement with a loud thud.

"Nigga, shut the fuck up!" Bino shot back.

"How much of a mu'fuck'n undercover do I look now!" Dez spat, standing there with blood across his face and a smoking .357 in his right hand.

Phenom looked at Dez, then turned towards Bino. He smiled wickedly, then said, "I like this nigga! Let's get down to business!"

* * *

Thursday
May 22, 2014
6:03 P.M.

Donell Jones played softly throughout each of Tahiry's Lacrosse speakers as she made a left onto Madison, snapping her fingers to the high of "Where I Wanna Be". The dudes on the corner of 18th Street and Avon standing in front of the old Mahogany's all the way down to Madison, were looking knowing it was her.

That's why Tah gave her money to tint her windows. He was overly protective of her as if they were together. Each of them had tried their hand with Tahiry and had been shot down.

She wasn't into dealing with dudes that were from her hood or around her family's house. Tah was just something she never planned on running into, but no matter how hard she tried, she couldn't shake him.

Everybody in that area knew the Lacrosse belonged to her because she was always parked on Madison. The young hustlers loved to see her pull up because they got to stare at her fat ass when she exited her car. As she pulled up in front of Tammy's house, Champ was climbing out of his new but used money green Ford Taurus LS. It was no secret that Champ had been in the worst of moods lately after getting shot. But since Tah had blessed him with $6,000, he had been smiling a lot more.

He was walking across the street as a brown Pontiac Grand AM rode down Madison playing Montell Jordan's "Get It On Tonight". He started bobbing his head, mouthing the lyrics to the song. Tah had not only given Champ money, but he gave Phenom and Doug the same amount. Doug then gave Doc half of hers for her role in the lick. Tah also gave Champ a kilo of both coke and dope, a pound of weed, and 1,000 ecstasy pills to do whatever he pleased.

He then put $7,000 towards China's medical bills and Vee and Tabi $1,000 for their pockets. He gave also Tahiry money to put on Mona, Lissa, and Chela's books then $20,000. Ten was for herself, the other half was to secure an exit investment.

He gave Tammy $2,000, Travis $500, and started bank accounts for Malani and Mya. He also gave Tahiry's mother, Mattie, $1,000. The two bank accounts he opened for his daughters had $2,500 in them. He was going to make sure his babies were good regardless.

He gave Mattie $4,000 to get him and Liz a house, too. There was no way he was about to let Tammy sign for it because she could be vindictive when she didn't get her way.

Tah had never had $75,000 all at once, but he knew that the next time that he got his hands on $70,000, he wasn't going to go through it in one day. After paying James Robbin $5,000 to pick up his and Phenom's cases, he bought Liz a $3,000 diamond bracelet. Then he was close to being broke again.

With his last $5,000, he gave Liz $3,500 for their dark red 2005 Chevrolet Tahoe which left him with $1,500. He put $1,000 to the side in his safe that he had Tahiry go out and buy for him, putting the last $500 in his pockets.

Tahiry double-parked next to Tah's Tahoe as Tah and Travis sat on the front porch. They were eating steamed shrimp. Tah wasn't much of a crab eater. He he didn't going through so much for so little meat. Tahiry climbed out of her Lacrosse in a green Gucci mini dress, and a pair of 6-inch Gucci stilettos.

"As salaamu alaikum," Champ greeted, walking up the steps.

"Wa alaikum as salaam," Tah and Travis returned, while both sat there peeling shells off of their shrimp before stuffing them into their mouths.

"Here," Tahiry said, walking up handing Tah the signed lease and a set of keys to their new house. "Your godmother said thank you and everything is set. Y'all could move in tonight if you want to."

"That's good to hear," Tah replied, nodding his head as three crack addicts walked past their house headed up to 18th Street to cop a hit.

"Tah, let me holla at you in the hallway real quick," Champ told him, standing there with his left arm in a sling.

"What the fuck we gotta go inside for? Talk nigga."

"I need you to come down to the Ville with me so I can set this shit up right."

127

"Man, take your scary ass down there and handle your shit."

"All that shit you talked about how you run through Millville, now you need help?" Tahiry laughed.

"Mind your business, Tahi," Champ said, turning back to Tah. "Just come down there once."

"I'll think about it. I gotta get shit right up here first."

"A'ight, just don't forget."

"Nigga, I ain't make no promise. I said I'll see."

"And I heard you mu'fucka."

"Yeah, a'ight," Tah said as Champ walked away. "What's up babygirl?"

"You do know Liz almost caught us yesterday, right?" Tahiry asked, looking at the two little girls next door.

"I had to see you. She'll be a'ight."

"Don't do that."

"What?" he asked, smiling.

"Try and sneak diss. You love Liz, so don't try and make it seem like it don't matter."

"Anyway, I'ma need you to take this trip with me in a few weeks."

"You know I got you," she said, sitting behind him on the steps. "I always got you."

CHAPTER 12
Saturday
May 31, 2014
10:00 a.m.

"What's up, nef? What you working with?" asked a tall white guy, wearing a Gulf Gas Station uniform on.

"A bitch got whatever a bitch need, nef. What the fuck you want?" Young replied, standing there in a brown Sean John flight jacket, a pair of dark blue True Religion jeans, and a pair of brown leather Timberlands.

"Let me get two thirties. What stamp you got?"

"Do Not Eat and Made In China," Young replied, as three teenage girls walked past watching him, knowing he was the next one to come up in the game underneath Bino.

"Oh, a'ight. You do got Do Not Eat. Let me get two bags," the dude told Young, pulling out a crumpled up hundred dollar bill, passing it to Young.

"Naw, nef. a bitch gotta go to nef over there, come on bruh, this ain't your mu'fuck'n first time," Young spat, nodding his head two houses down where Glee was at, sitting on the porch. "Stop acting all stupid and shit, nef!"

"That's my bad, bro. I just figured you had it. I'm just running late and my boss is a real asshole! One day I was running a little late and he had the nerve to tell a bitch tha—"

"Bruh! Take your mu'fuck'n ass down there and get your shit! I don't give a fuck about you and your boss!" Young snapped, as Rico pulled up in Silver Chevrolet Impala LS with his brother Fleche sitting in the passenger seat smoking a blunt of sour diesel.

"Young, what's poppin, nef?" Rico asked, watching the fiend walk towards Glee.

"What's good, nigga. What the fuck y'all doing over here on this end?"

"I had to meet one of my fiends around the corner at JoJo's, so I figured I'd come see what was up with Bino bitch ass."

"That nigga ain't out here. You gotta catch him and Rah in the afternoon," Young told him as another fiend walked up to him.

"A'ight, let a bitch know that I came through," Rico said, rolling his window back up and pulling away from the curb without waiting for Young to respond.

Sixteen-year old Kendal "Young" Nicks watched Rico's Impala pull off as two more fiends walked up to him looking for the dope. They wanted the ones stamped Do Not Enter and Made In China. They needed to get their hands on that new dope Tah sent down with Phenom. Young's girlfriend 18-year old, Dime, was coming from Up Top also known as East State Street with her bestfriend, Mama. Both came from Georgia's Chicken Shack.

Young already knew what Dime wanted. See, since Phenom pulled up with the dope stamped Do Not Enter and Made In China, Da Section had been turned into the walking dead. All of the zombie looking fiends dragged about all doped up around there.

Fiends have been crawling from high and low to get to Da Section to sample the new phenomenon that Bino put his stamp of approval on, causing talk throughout Trenton. He and Rah were positioned on South Walter Avenue just off of the corner of Walnut Avenue. The block was ran by a dude name Raye who had been out there for years now.

Raye respected Bino and Rah's hustle because they showed him they could handle their own without involving him in it. Plus, they bought the most work from him out of everybody on the block. After Phenom came into town with the new pipeline for Bino, Raye saw less of Bino's money. His work wasn't moving anymore after Bino put Tah's coke and dope out there.

Bino's crew consisted of him, Rah, Young, Dez, and now Glee who had just started working for him after he saw the flood his new pipeline was dishing out. Glee used to work for Raye. That was the thing to do lately, but Bino wasn't taking anymore workers.

Every one of Raye's young boys was trying to get a piece of the action. After seeing all the traffic on the corner of Walnut Avenue, they all wanted to get with the winning team. It didn't help they weren't seeing money the way they did before Phenom stepped foot into Trenton.

Tah wasn't what he was doing when he bagged up the bricks of dope. He just sent it down there, filling each bag to the top. Bino took those bricks and broke them down, re-bagging them.

Bino bagged up sixteen bricks and the bags were still fat and heavy. The samples turned into a quick flip. Rah cooked the coke up, stretching twenty grams into thirty-eight grams. He let Rah know the coke was straight drop, nearly 100% pure.

When it was all said and done, Bino and Rah were looking to bring back nearly $15,000 from both, the crack and dope, alike. Tah didn't ask for anything, giving it to Phenom as samples so the could unload his work in Trenton. However, he and Bino had other plans with the work. Phenom was taking $5,000 while Bino was splitting $10,000 with his team. He gave Dez three bricks for himself to take to Camden to get the buzz popping down there.

Bino had left Young and Glee with two bricks of dope and five grams of crack bagged up in 30's. The rest of the work he had with him as he rode around with Leo in her red Honda Accord making his drop offs. Bino had been spending a lot of time with Leo because she was his driver while he unloaded his work throughout Trenton.

Young and Glee, however, held down Da Section. Shay didn't have much to say because she was compensated. Bino had giving her $5,000 over the past few weeks now that he had extra money to blow. She didn't protest because she was in the mall going crazy.

Shay wasn't the only one tearing up the clothing stores and nail salons. Dime was seeing more and more of South Walter Avenue since Phenom hit Bino with the goodness. Dime was from Chambersburg, but she'd been coming over to Da Section to empty Young's pockets. He'd been seeing more money lately, too since Bino was taking care of his workers.

Dime was wearing a pair of gold and black Jimmy Choo sneakers, a black and gold G-Star starter jacket, and a pair of Ferragamo jeans. Young had been getting endless pussy from his girlfriend because his pockets had gotten deeper.

"Hey, baby. What you doin'?" Dime asked, leaning in and giving Young a kiss with a little bit of tongue.

"I'm in the trap, Dime. What do you think a bitch doing!" Young shot back, wondering how long before she stuck her hand out.

"Why you gotta be so nasty about it?"

"What do you want, Dime? You know I don't like it when you're on the block while I'm grinding."

"Yo, hit nef up and let him know that we done with everything," Glee informed, walking up and putting a smile on Dime's face with the information he just gave Young.

"A'ight, I'm about to hit bruh right now. He probably riding around somewhere," Young replied, before turning to

Dime and noticing the smile on her face. "What the fuck you smiling for?"

"If y'all don't got no more shit, I know you got some money," Dime told him, not ashamed of how thirsty she might have looked in his eyes.

"I ain't got no money right now, so if that's why you walked all the way over here, then you just wasted your time!"

Whoop! Whoop!

"Everybody up against the car!" Detective Copeland ordered, hopping out of the state-issued navy blue Dodge Caliber before it could come to a complete stop.

"Shit!" Glee gasped, walking towards the white Mitsubishi Eclipse that was parked in front of them.

"Uh uh, where do y'all think that y'all going? Get the fuck over here and put your hands on the hood!" Detective Federals snapped after climbing out of the Caliber. Dime and Mama tried to walk off as if they didn't know Young and Glee.

"We didn't do nothing!" Mama yelled.

"Yeah, yeah, yeah. That's what they all say. For all I know, you could be the one holding the work," Detective Federals returned, shoving Mama in her back, forcing her against the hood of the Eclipse.

"What's up, Nicks? What do you got for me today?" Detective Copeland asked, patting Young's front pockets hoping to find some drugs. "Do you have anything sharp in your pockets?"

"Naw, I ain't got shit. You know I don't, so I don't know why you're fuck'n with me," Young replied, lifting his head to cut his eyes at Detective Copeland.

"I guess I'm bored. Now shut up and keep your head down!"

"Come on, Copeland, man. A bitch ain't did nothing, man!" Glee informed.

"That's what your mouth say. What do you know about that kid that got killed over there the other week?"

"We don't know shit," Young replied.

* * *

2:38 p.m. In Atlantic City, New Jersey

"Speak on it," Soo said into his iPhone 3S, turning the radio of his phantom black Porsche Panamera S sedan as he sat on New York Avenue.

"I think I found a lead about who hit us," Pont replied, sitting in the passenger seat of his black-purple Chrysler Pacifica, which was parked on Clinton Avenue and 11ᵗʰ Street.

"Handle your business. The order came down that you're to wipe any and everything out that was close to that house," Soo told Pont as he turned his head to his left and spotted his young girl, Zoey, walking out of her house. "I'll see you in a few days."

"How am I supposed to do this?"

"It doesn't matter. Just get the shit done before I get back, the sooner the better."

"Say no more," Pont replied, before hanging up on Soo.

Though Soo was inside of his Panamera S by himself, there were two midnight black Chrysler Pacificas following him everywhere he went. Inside of each Pacifica were four heavily armed gunmen that were licensed to carry. All of Soo's hired help was paid $2,500 a week to protect and/or die for him as if he were Jahad.

Jahad made sure that everybody understood that what Soo said was law and if you went against him, then you went against him and that came with death. A few had already lost their lives behind that law alone. Jahad had built another empire with the help of Soo, and they were going hard with no plans of stopping any time soon.

Zoey climbed into the Panamera S, sliding into the confines of the soft sakhir orange leather seats with Tiburon grey accents throughout them, looking like a caramel toned Paula Patton. She leaned over and kissed Soo on his right cheek. He smiled as the dudes standing on the block looked on with envy. Since Soo had been fucking Zoey, she had been greatly upgraded to the point that even she had to question if it was really real.

Soo had come and saved this girl from the gutter of Atlantic City. She knew she would still be sitting around trying to game dudes for a few dollars, or even waiting around for a welfare check every month if it hadn't been for him. So, whatever Soo told her to do or asked of her, she would do with the biggest smile on her face. She was grateful to have a dude like him in her life, even if she wasn't number one.

As Soo put the Panamera S into drive, Zoey looked over at him with lust. She had to take a deep breath at his nearly perfect appearance. Soo was wearing a $6,500 Peak Lapel plum Muhair stripe Tom Ford suit with a pair of $2,000 black Gianni leather cap toe Chelsea Tom Ford boots. On his left wrist was a $42,000 18-karat rose gold Tutima Patria watch with a Opaline silver dial and plum alligator strap.

Zoey couldn't stop herself from smiling, sitting there in a $5,000 full length black ankle, hugging Brunello Cucinelli short sleeve dress that he bought her for tonight. In her ears were two-karat diamond studs that cost him $8,000 a piece, and on her right wrist was a $3,500 one and a half karat diamond bracelet. Zoey leaned over and kissed him on his cheek again and said, "Hey, daddy. I didn't have you waiting too long, did I?"

"Nah, you know you're always on time for me," Soo returned, causing her to smile as he handed her his chrome .45 caliber that was sitting on his lap.

"I'm so lucky."

"Are you now?" Soo replied, pulling away from the curb as he turned on R. Kelly's "Bump and Grind" back on.

See I know just what you want and I know just what you
need girl
so baby bring your body to me (bring your body here)
I'm not fooling around with you
Baby my love is true, with you
(With you is where I want to be) is where, I wanna be
Girl you need someone, someone like me to satisfy your
every needs

* * *

7:30 p.m. In Trenton

"I talked to nef and a bitch about to have that drop by the boatload," Bino informed, standing next to his white Chevrolet Impala SS. He was in his buttercream soft leather Pelle Pelle jacket, a pair of blue Buffalo jeans, and a pair of tan Timberlands.

"What about the situation with nef?" Young asked, standing in front of Bino with Glee to his left.

"Fuck that nigga!" Rah barked as two fiends walked up all buggy-eyed, thirsty for a blast of crack. "A bitch been out this bitch just as long as the next! We ain't about to go nowhere! What the fuck we supposed to do? Stop feeding our family 'cause his pockets looking light?"

"That's what I'm saying. I told nef he gotta understand that a bitch ain't tryna cut his throat," Glee added, standing there smoking a blunt. "A bitch down to ride until that nigga casket drops!"

"Fuck it. I say we ride out on them niggas tonight, nef!" Rah said, ready to turn Da Section into a war zone over a dollar.

"Fuck it, I'm down!" Young jumped in.

A war right now wasn't what Bino needed and, in fact, it would be the very last thing he needed. The block was just starting to die down from the murder Dez committed weeks ago. Bino wasn't afraid to go to battle with Raye and his crew. He just knew they were outnumbered and outgunned right now and a war would probably be a slaughter.

He just had to win his crew over with understanding because he had a lot on the line. Phenom was bringing down some more work in the next couple of days, so he needed everything to be lined up and ready for this shipment. Phenom talked Tah into letting him to come down with a big shipment of both coke and dope. With that, Bino was going to start building his empire.

"Everybody calm down and hear me out. With this shipment coming down in a couple of days, a bitch gotta be smart about this shit. Making a move tonight ain't a good idea."

"Don't tell me that you're scared to go get at these mu'fu—"

"A bitch ain't scared of shit!" Bino snapped, turning to face Rah as he cut him off in mid-sentence. "I said that shit ain't a good move. We don't even know if Raye said the shit. Y'all niggas going off on what another nigga said."

"Bino, we can't let this nigga think that we soft. We gotta make a statement before it's too late," Rah replied as a grey Jeep Compass turned the corner behind a red Dodge Magnum.

"Ain't nobody gon' think we sof—"

Tat, tat, tat, tat, tat, tat, tat, tat, tat, tat, tat, tat, tat, tat!

Just as the words left Bino's mouth, a parade of AK-47 bullets came shooting their way tagging up his Impala. The four of them hit the deck with the reflex of a cat. Rah reached into his waistline and grabbed his black glock 9-millimeter, quickly looking under the Impala for the cause of the attack.

Bino pulled out his chrome .45 caliber, looking over at Young and Glee didn't pulling out anything because they weren't strapped. That was a big mistake. He shook his head and opened his eyes wider to see better. The reality hit him like ton of a bricks.

Glee hadn't hit the ground because of the shots. He hit the ground because he'd been shot, a bullet taking half of his face off the moment they started shooting. Shattered glass fell on top of them as the shots continued to rain down on them.

Kids dropped to the ground with their trick or treat bags, trying not to get hit or lose any candy. Young locked eyes with Bino exposing that he too had been hit, a chunk of his left arm was missing. A tear slowly rolled down Young's cheek as he stared at him.

Rah was just waiting for his chance to do some damage but the AK-47 seemed to never run out of bullets. What took mere seconds felt like years to end. Debris and glass covered the air like mist, surrounding them as Bino tried to find an opening to return fire. He closed his eyes for two seconds, then he hopped up and dashed towards the back of his Impala while still ducking.

As he cleared the Impala, he raised his .45 and pulled the trigger, sending bullets into the back window of the Compass, freeing Rah up to get in on the action.

Rah hopped up and the moment he did, he locked eyes with Raye's little brother who was in the passenger seat of the Compass. He was enraged to the point that he started shooting wildly. The back passenger was shooting at Bino, giving Rah the split second he needed to aim and shoot sufficiently.

Boc! Boc! Boc! Boc! Boc!

Scccccuuurrrrr!

Boc! Bloc! Boc! Bloc! Bloc!

The Compass peeled away from the scene with tire screeching force. Bino and Rah chased behind them, shooting and hitting the jeep in different places as it recklessly shot up South Walter Avenue. Everybody on the block lied down on the ground in the cut, behind cars, on the side of houses, and next to people's porches, all in sheer terror. Da Section had always been a rough section out of all of the neighborhoods in Trenton, but after what had just happened, it added another notch to the madness.

Rah turned his head toward Bino with his gun dangling at his side, the barrel still smoking as police sirens roared loudly in a distance.. His chest heaving up and down with raging adrenaline, he angrily said, "Fuck what you talking about! This shit just got real!"

"Fuck real, it's fuck'n war!"

* * *

Wednesday
June 4, 2014
7:35 p.m. In Camden

"Rob Bino, what's poppin', my nigga?" Dez greeted, answering his red iPhone 3S while standing on the corner of Mechanic Street in front of the grocery store facing Rose Street.

"A bitch 'bout to come to C.M.D. for a few days, nef," Bino replied as he sat on his couch in his living room watching

State Property. Shay was lying on the couch with her head resting on his lap.

"No-Fronts, bring me four bags," Dez's little brother, Temp, ordered as he stood in the doorway of the corner store with two dope addicts standing behind him.

"Why, what's good?" Dez anxiously asked, thinking Bino was bringing him more dope. "You must be bringing that jawn down here with you."

"Nah, shit just got real out here. Niggas tried to roll on us, so a bitch need to lay low for a min—"

"Fuck you mean niggas tried to roll on y'all?" Dez shot back as Buzzy rode up on a 10-speed Huffy bike. "Nigga, me and lil' bruh about to come up there! What the fuck would you come down here for if the problem is up there?"

"What's good, Temp, with your weak ass?" Buzzy greeted, hopping off of his bike as Dez rudely hung up on Bino.

"Uncle Buzz, what's up with your dusty ass?" Temp shot back as No-Fronts served the two fiends.

"Dusty?" Buzzy replied, looking from Temp to No-Fronts. "Nigga, y'all out here popped, wishing you could fuck that bag up like me!"

"Tim, let's roll. We got some shit to handle real quick," Dez said, walking towards Temp's brown Chevrolet Malibu.

Temp wasted no time walking towards his car. Whenever Dez spoke, Temp followed. He reached the passenger side and climbed into the car as Dez started the engine. Temp looked at him and asked, "What's the word?"

"Work!"

Already understanding what that meant, Temp grabbed his gun and cocked a bullet into the chamber, then replied, "That's what I like to hear! Let's ride!"

CHAPTER 13
Tuesday
June 17, 2014
10:00 P.M. Roselle, New Jersey

9 o' clock (9 o' clock)
All alone (all alone)
Paging you (paging you)
Wishing you come over
My place (my place)
after a while (after a while)
Let me know (let me know)

As Ginuwine was pouring his soul out on his hit classic "So Anxious", Liz was crying her soul out in her own pleasurable way. The music was softly flowing through the Panasonic surround sound system that cornered off their bedroom, bouncing sound from wall to wall. She was laying on her stomach on their plush California king size bed covered with 500 count thread sheets. Her face was buried in the three-in-one plush pillows she'd gotten from Bed, Bath, & Beyond.

Liz had both of her hands tightly clenched into fists with Tah's hands covering hers. Their fingers locked and intertwined passionately. He lied on top of her, slowly entering her with concentrated, stomach touching strokes, grinding his hips to the majestic rhythm of the music.

With each drenching, pussy wall gripping thrust he administrated, she tightened her eyes even harder, releasing moans of ecstasy and pleasure. Liz was meeting each of his hip crushing strokes with thirsty thrust of her own, never wanting the feeling she was experiencing to come to an end.

Said it's 10:10 (10:10)
Where you been (where you been)

Did you get my message (get my message)
Your expressions is telling me
That you've been thinking the same thing (same thing)
I've been thinking

"Ooooh, bae! Yes!" Liz moaned intensely, her toes curling into a grip as he pulled his dick out of her leaving the head. "Please don't. Please, bae. Give it, give it to me. Please, mmmmmm."

"Damn, girl," Tah shot back, hungrily biting down on his bottom lip. He closed his eyes appreciatively, savoring the feeling that ignited through the striking of her wet walls contracting around his erection. "Got damn, I love being inside of you."

"Aahhhh, oooohh. Please, give it to me! Give me my dick!"

"You want this dick?" he replied in a soft Tyrese bedroom voice as his sweat dropped from his forehead onto her back. He then inched further into her warm pussy.

"Ooohh, yes, daddy," Liz moaned, trying to push her ass against him, attempting to suck his whole dick into her pussy. "Please, give me my dick, daddy. I need it!"

"Mmmmmm," Tah groaned with a therapeutic poise in his stroke, the passion oozing out. "How bad do you want this dick?"

"Mmmmmmm, I—I," she stuttered just as Tah stroked deeply inside of her, sending chills down her spine. He pulled his dick back out of her pussy and looked down at her creamy nectar that glazed the length of his dick. He slowly stuck the head back in, then pulled it back out only to slide it back in, causing Liz to whine. "P—please! Please, daddy! O—oooohh m—my fuck'n, ooohh!"

142

"Tell me how bad you want this dick," Tah whispered, arching his back as he grinded the head of his dick in and out of her tight pussy.

"T—Tahiem, p—please, b—baby!"

Leaning in as he gently nibbled on Liz's left earlobe before sucking on it, Tah softly licked her neck. He brought his lips within centimeters of her ear and said, "I said tell daddy how fuck'n bad you want this fuck'n dick, bitch!"

"Oooohh, I-I-I want. I want it, daddy. Ooohh, I. Aahhh, ah, aah. Oooh, I fuck'n n-n-need it!" Liz screamed fiendishly as Usher's "Nice & Slow", replacing "So Anxious" which caused him to switch up his stroke pattern.

"Oh, you need it, huh?"

"Yes, yes, yes! I fuck'n need it!" she screamed, turning her head to the right with a mean scowl on her face, while he deeply thrusted into her drowning wet pussy as she slowly raised her body.

With Tah's guidance, Liz eased her body back. Her knees cemented into the confines of the mattress with her ass high in the air, spread eagle as she leaned forward on her elbows. Liz turned her head to the left, locking her eyes with Tah's as they exchanged an intimate stare. Both spoke so many silent words that only they understood.

Tah held her tightly by her 26-inch waist steadily grinding his hips, stroking her hypnotically with the fiendish concentration of an addict. If words could grab a hold of his to express the pleasure he was feeling right now, they would release say "damn".

Tah was stroking in and out of Liz so slowly, matching the drums and break down to the beat of "Nice & Slow". Liz's back quickly gave out as drool dribbled from her bottom lip, numb from the stroke he delivered that released her flow of nectar.

I'm, I'm—fuck!" Liz screamed out, pulling a pillow towards her face. She bit down into it and growled, "I'm cuummmmming!"

"Yeah, that's right," Tah said, stroking even harder as he felt her pussy grow wetter, her walls violently contracted around his dick. "Cum all over this dick."

"Aaaggghhhhh!" she bellowed out, as he leaned forward with his left arm wrapped around her midsection, vigorously rubbing her clit in a circular rotation. He intensified her orgasm that as he continued to hit her with long dick, slow strokes, maiming the pussy.

I wanna do something freaky to you, babe
I don't think they heard me
I-I wanna do something freaky to you, babe
To call out my name
They call me U-S-H-E-R R-A-Y-M-O-N-D
Now baby tell me what you wanna do with me

Liz was trying to run from the extreme chaotic sensation from the combination of her climax and the premeditated strokes of each of his thrust. Tah continued to rub her clit with thirsty, thunderous circular thrusts, causing her eyes to roll into the back of her head while her body experienced slight trembles.

He could feel the hairs on the back of his neck stand up, while his toes gripped the bottom of his feet, goosebumps engulfing his body. Ever since he had proposed to her, their sex life and lovemaking had been overly intense. It was like her pussy became more fruitful to him, causing him to crave it even more, even ejaculating deep inside of her. After filling her insides with his semen, Tah laid on top Liz who was breathing hard as he held her tightly.

Tah had moved his family out to Roselle in a four-bedroom one family house on 4th Avenue and Spruce Street.

It was him, Liz, Mya, Malani, and Travis. He made the decision to take his little brother with them, giving Tammy some much needed time for herself. He figured he was already taking care of him anyway.

It took a day or two for Tah's new lawyer, James Robbin, to get the judge to agree to an address change, but he made it happen. Liz had been buying furniture for the house every day since they had moved in. She was spending the money just as fast as he was making it.

Doug and Jerm were buying a nice amount of the work from him, while cutting GK out of the picture completely. Tah's prices were ten times better and the work was twenty times better than GK's. Doug, Jerm, Tabi, and Vee were moving so much work, they hadn't even realized they'd moved over 300 grams of coke, making them come back more and more. Doc started moving dope up on Madison Avenue, just doors down from Tammy's house with the help of Phenom's peoples, Phantom and Known.

All together, Liz had spent $10,000 on furnishing their house, leaving Tah with a little over $15,000 in his safe. Liz and Tahiry stayed inside of Lowes, IKEA, Unclaimed Freight, and Bed, Bath, & Beyond, picking out different pieces to make their home feel like home.

Tahiry was buying furniture for her little studio apartment that Tah helped her get. He was paying his sister for handling his money whenever it came in. Travis was enjoying being out of the hood and the school he was going to. He couldn't remember the last time he was this happy.

He had made friends out there rather quickly and wasn't worrying about getting shot while playing basketball or football at the park. He could actually be kid for once and not worry about anything. Though he would always worry about Tammy, he didn't have to be around her all day, every day watching her slowly kill herself by drinking. Tah had removed him from all of that.

Shit is all over the news
Bomb goes off in Central
What the fuck have I gotten myself into
The mental is like get the fuck outta there
I'm out
Hey, going somewhere
Nah
What's your bags for for
Fuck it what you want
Can your nigga come inside for a minute and puff a blunt
Here we go again
After what I just gave you
You wasn't acting like this when you ask for that favor

"As salaamu alaikum," Tah greeted, answering his new white iPhone 3S, cutting DMX's ringtone "Damien 2" featuring Marilyn Manson short.

"Wa alaikum as salaam, Okhi," both Champ and Phenom returned.

"What's good?"

"Shit is crazy right now. I need to link up with you, bruh. Bino been beating my phone down for days now," Phenom informed as he lied next to Chrissy in her plush queen size bed.

"Word up. I got BH and Meer calling me like I owe them something. Plus, I got a few niggas in Millville that's tryna dance," Champ jumped in, sitting in the passenger seat of his Taurus rolling a blunt of 189th in a vanilla dutch.

"I can understand Phenom needing me, but Champ, what the fuck happened to all of the shoes I gave you?" Tah questioned as Liz rolled over and grabbed her phone to check her Facebook page.

"It's a long story, but I'm walking around in socks out here now."

"Damn, nigga! What the fuck, son!"

"Well I don't know about this backwards ass nigga, but my shoes are in need of repair," Phenom said as Chrissy turned around and wrapped his arm around her.

"A'ight, give me a few hours. I'll have Tahi send y'all some new Jordans."

"A'ight, bet. That's what's up," Phenom replied excitedly. "And I'm coming up there to holla at you about something else after I lace my Jordans."

"Say no more. I need you to come up anyway because Mr. Robbin wants to handle that situation with you and that questioning shit," Tah told him as Liz walked into their master bedroom bathroom, while liking posts and reposting other posts.

"Good looking, bruh. I'ma give sis that bread for my sneakers when they get here," Champ said, preparing to hang up.

"Don't mention it. We all we got."

"As salaamu alaikum," Phenom said.

"Wa alaikum as salaam," Tah and Champ responded before the three of them disconnected their call.

"So, I guess Doc and Tabi gon' be hitting the road again, huh?" Liz said, poking her head out of the bathroom.

"There you go minding grown folks business again," Tah shot back at her as he pulled Facebook up on his phone and began scrolling down his newsfeed.

"Excuse me, I didn't know that it was such a secret!"

"Come on now, Liz. You know better than to question me about that shit. I keep my family and business completely separate."

"Whatever, but you got Tahi and the crew all in your shit, though."

"Liz, this shit ain't up for debate. We're not having this conversation, so just leave it alone. You're my wife to be and there are just things I choose not to involve you in, period."

"Alright, Tahiem! Got damn!" she spat, slamming the bathroom door.

"If it's alright, then what the fuck you got an attitude for?"

* * *

Monday
June 23, 2014
11:13 a.m. In Newark

"Your Honor, Mr. Muhammad was present at the scene of the crime the day in question. We have reason to believe that he was involved if not one of the shooters," Prosecutor Karl Anthony stated, standing behind the defense table looking down at his stack of tan folders which were his caseloads.

"So what charges have the state brought up against the defendant because I don't see anything here that warrants a shooting or murder?" Judge Francois asked, looking down at the prosecutor.

Prosecutor Anthony brushed some imaginary lint off of the shoulder of his grey fitted JCME two-piece suit. He looked up at the judge then replied, "At this moment, we haven't filed any charges relating to this crime. However, we do believe th—"

"So what I'm hearing is that the state is asking me to continue to hold Mr. Muhammad accountable for a charge that just doesn't exist?" Judge Francois replied, turning towards Tah.

"Ummm, that's not the case, your honor. We're just asking that you give us a little more because, at the moment, we're looking to grab his accomplice and question him. In the meantime, we do have Mr. Muham—"

"Your Honor, my client has spent the last four weeks on house arrest after sitting in the county for six and a half months because the state doesn't know where their case begins to bring it to an end," James Robbin said, standing there in a peach and cream pinstripe Yah-Yah Baby business suit.

"I'm well aware of the position your client has been in. However, Mr. Muhammad has been on house arrest because of the weapons charges filed against him," Judge Francois informed, moving the paper to the side that was sitting in front of him so that he could look at Tah's charges.

"Yes, your Honor. And about those charges," James Robbin replied, also flipping the pages in front of him to the left. "My firm has sent you a copy of the discovery and a copy of the statements by every person present when my client was arrested. Mr. Muhammad didn't in fact have a weapon on him nor did he put up any type of resistance."

"That's not what the arresting detective reported," Prosecutor Anthony said, causing the judge to look at James Robbin who was holding a stack of papers in the air in his right hand with his left hand on the table.

"I have here a written statements from every student in that classroom as well as the security guard that watched my client be placed in the police vehicle."

"Mr. Anthony?"

Prosecutor Anthony sat down in his seat with a defeated expression on his face. He looked over the statements the bailiff had just handed him and the judge. He was clearly blindsided by the evidence he had delivered today. He wiped his face with his left and right hand, then admitted, "The state was not aware of this, I assure you."

Judge Francois was upset about the time the prosecution had wasted instead of doing their job. He wasn't sure if Tah was guilty and at the rate that Prosecutor Anthony was going, he'd would never know. With nothing else to hold him on, Judge Francois had no choice but to dismiss all of the charges, ordering the bailiff to cut the ankle bracelet off of Tah's leg.

Liz sat in the audience with the biggest smile on her face expressing just how happy she was. She knew they could now go places after not being able to, to enjoy their newfound wealth together. James Robbin stood there collecting his papers as he prepared to stuff them into the dark brown Gucci briefcase that sat next to his left foot. He was satisfied with the outcome of today's proceedings.

Once the bracelet was cut off of his ankle, Tah leaned over and rubbed his it. Then he stood up and smiled at the judge before turning towards James Robbin. He gave him a huge hug for a job well done.

He then told him how much he appreciated his efforts, giving him $10,000. He told him he would drop the rest of his money off tomorrow when his office opened. He shook his hand once again, then strutted over to his woman. Liz was standing there with the saddest expression on her face until he wrapped his arms around her. He started kissing her all over her face, putting a smile on it that not even death could take away.

Tah stepped out of the courthouse on High Street, wearing a blue and black Brooks Brother double breasted suit with a pair of brown $800 Clarks on his feet. James Robbin came walking out of the courthouse, telling told Tah to have Phenom come to his office so they could go down to homicide and clear his name. Altogether, James Robbin had made $25,000 off of Tah with more still to come.

Tah was about to really get down to business because he had a lot of work to move. He had Phenom down in Trenton, Champ down Millville, Doc and Phantom on Madison, and his favorite white boy, Dave M. down in Wildwood, New Jersey. He was taking a trip down to Trenton to finally meet Bino before going down to Millville.

Champ was now on the payroll after fucking up the work that Tah had given him. Somehow or another, Champ managed to go to Millville and fuck up everything he got from him. When he should've made over $100,000 plus, Champ had barely made $60,000. He had to give Tah $45,000 up front for the work Tah had sent him when he and Phenom called the other day telling him that they were dry.

He got beat for a lot of it because nobody took him seriously, then he blew a lot of money trying to floss for everybody. Champ wouldn't admit it to his boy, but he didn't know what he was doing. He was done dirty by a few hustlers down there, thinking he could do it without their help.

James Robbin promised Tah that Phenom wasn't going to be arrested for anything because they had no weapon. A fingerprint on a bullet only said that Phenom touched the bullet. It didn't say he had the gun or if he'd shot the gun. And until they could prove that, they could only question him and release him.

However, he needed to get him to the precinct and get things over with before the situation worsened. With China still in a coma, the police didn't had any evidence against him to try and charge him with murder.

"Where do you wanna go first?" Liz asked Tah, smiling harder than him when he was the one who had the charges dropped.

Grabbing the door handle of their Tahoe, she stopped to think about it, then replied, "Dragon Fly!"

* * *

Down in Trenton

"What you working with, youngin?" Mrs. Cody asked, walking up on Raye's little brother, Todd, who stood next to three of Raye's workers.

"We got that fire, What you need?" Todd asked her.

"Do y'all got Made In China?"

"What the fuck you ask me, bitch!"

"Yo, nef! Chill out! That's my man's grandmother, bruh," Hood stated, stepping to Todd know about how he was out of pocket, talking to the older lady in that manner.

"I don't give a fuck who she is, coming over here asking about some mu'fuck'n Made In China!" Todd snapped, turning around to stare Hood down, even with him being taller than him.

"Bruh, you act like she know what's out here. The woman just asking a question," Wark joined in, shaking his head from right to left with disappointment.

"She comes here every fuck'n day copping dope from us. She knows we don't sell that shit that they selling down the street," Todd expressed, revealing his frustrations and anger about Bino and Rah's departure from their operation.

"Mrs. Cody, I'm sorry about this nigga's disrespect. Nah, we don't have that stamp over here," Hood told her, stepping closer so he could wrap his arm around her. He turned her in the opposite direction and started walking her down towards Young and Temp.

"Harold, you shouldn't be around people like that. You gon' end up in a situation you shouldn't be in," Mrs. Cody informed, grateful that her grandson was respected enough in the streets that she was protected by some.

"I know, I know," he replied, thinking about what Bino had said to him the other day.

Dez and Temp had come into Trenton carrying a storm on their backs, ready to knock every one of Raye's people off, but Bino wanted things done right. He wasn't running to Camden to hide, but more so to let the heat die down.

After Todd and his boys shot at them on Halloween, Bino and Rah had shot up three of Raye's spots and killed two of his runners. Doc and Tabi had brought 500 grams of coke and 300 bricks of dope down to Trenton for Phenom who, in return, sold half of it to Bino for half the money up front.

Bino and Rah put their money together and gave Phenom $15,000 for 250 grams of coke and 150 bricks of dope. Phenom took his $5,000 and gave Doc $10,000 to take back to Tah.

Now with more work that would bring them back more money, Bino felt it was time to step his game up and take over Raye's whole operation one runner at a time. That's why he approached Hood and Wark to work for him.

Wark said no, but Hood told him he had to think about it. He knew his bills had to get paid. Then, on top of that, he had known Bino for a few years now, respecting him a little bit more than he respected Raye.

Glee was dead and was scheduled to be buried in a couple of days. Young was back out there, but his left arm was in a cast, so Dez told Bino it was time to build their army up and acquire more numbers. Dez had come in and took control of the position of army commander with Temp by his side. He was dropping niggas left and right.

Trenton's murder rate shot through the roof in the last few days with six people being gunned down in broad daylight.

Dez just didn't give a fuck! Police were on high alert, but they had no clue as to where to begin. With Dez not being from out there, it was kind of hard for them to finger their killer. Bino told Dez to try and keep the shootings out of Da Section, so he tried to catch niggas elsewhere. But at the end of the day, he was shooting niggas wherever he caught them.

As Hood reached the corner of Walnut Avenue, he witnessed Rah sitting shotgun in a tan Audi S4 with a blue bandana wrapped around his face. His heart dropped knowing he'd been caught slipping right now trying to help his man's grandmother.

However, the S4 kept driving up South Walter Avenue without conviction. Dez drove at a normal speed so he didn't attract the wrong attention. Hood looked back one time before continued on. He was thankful he wasn't up the street because even Ray Charles could see what was about to happen.

Todd stood there yelling at Wark and Terrance about the drugs Bino had out there on their strip. He had to let his frustrations go somehow or another. Raye decided he didn't want Todd out there on the front line throwing himself into the war head first.

He told him to fall back and focus on the money, leaving the killing to him. Todd was mad about that, but he knew better than to go up against his big brother. So he was on the block everyday taking it out on the runners.

"Y'all mu'fuckas better act like y'all know what this shit is out here. A bitch ain't sharing shit with them niggas down there!' Todd snapped with his back against the street.

"Nef, we ain't beat for that shit you talking. At the end of the day, you just don't talk to nobody grandmother like that," Terrance replied, preparing to walk off as the S4 pulled up behind Todd.

"Aye, yo, nef!" Rah yelled from the passenger seat.

"What, mu'fuck—" Todd started to say, spinning around to see Rah aiming his glock 9-millmenter at him with a wicked smile on his face. "Shit!"

"Yeah, pussy!" Dez laughed as Wark and Terrance turned to run, while Todd froze up at the sight of a gun.

Boc! Boc! Boc! Boc! Boc! Boc!

* * *

Back Up North

"So, how does it feel to be out with your baby again?" Liz asked, looking over at Tah as he drove down Route 19, crossing South Wood Avenue.

"It feels regular. Nothing really spectacular about being out with somebody I see everyday," Tah joked, cutting his eye at her as he waited for her reaction.

"Fuck you mean regular? Nigga, don't get your shit split before we get up in here!" Liz shot back, turning her whole body towards him, while he leaned on the passenger door. "I'll have your ass walking up in Dragonfly looking like Tina after Ike beat that ass in the limo on their way to the hotel!"

"That shit sound gangsta as hell, but you missing one part."

"What?"

"Tina fucked Ike up in that limo before they got to the hotel."

"I can't stand your dumb ass!" she laughed, shoving Tah playfully and turning back around.

"I know, but you love it, though," he said and smiled, looking over to his left at the Hampton Inn that sat next to the AMC in the Aviation Plaza. He turned his head towards Liz and smiled even harder with much wickedness.

"Nigga, bye. We have a home where we can do whatever, whenever, however, and wherever we want to for free!"

"I'm saying, it's the experience that comes with it. Checking in and getting room service and shit," he said.

"Yeah, well we can go home after we eat. I'll stand at the front door with my iPad and act like I'm checking you in. Then I'll walk you up to our bedroom and let you in with a key. I'll put on my shortest skirt and play room service, then come in and fuck your brains out. You can give me all that money that you was gonna pay them!"

"For real?"

"Hell yeah."

"A'ight, fuck Dragonfly, We going home right now!" Tah replied, turning the wheel away from the direction of Dragonfly, looking like he was in a rush.

"Tahiem, stop playing! I'm hungry!" Liz yelled, slapping him on his right arm.

"Shit, don't talk to me like that 'cause I was ready to see how nasty you was gon' be as housekeeping!" Tah laughed, turning and parking in front of Applebee's where he found an open parking space.

"Oh, trust, I can get real fuck'n nasty in my skimpy lil' skirt," she seductively whispered in his ear, causing his dick to shoot for the moons.

"If you're as hungry as you say you are, you better stop talking to me like that!" he replied, grabbing a hand full of his erect dick through his jeans.

Liz was so excited to be going out with her boo after not being able to enjoy going places with him since being in a committed relationship. Then to top everything off, Tah was getting more money than he had ever seen and he couldn't even enjoy spending it with her. So the money started not to mean anything to him because of that. Now, he was free and ready to explore different things with his lady, and needless to say, she was all for it.

Tah climbed out of the Tahoe wearing a plum color JCME linen suit with a pair of Clarks on his feet. On his left wrist, he had a platinum presidential Rolex that Liz had picked out for him. She was wearing a cream color Fendi spaghetti strap mini dress with a pair of red wine, four-inch Fendi stilettos, and a red and cream Fendi handbag. Her hair was hanging down freely to the left side, showing off the tattoo on her neck.

They walked up to Dragonfly hand in hand, talking about small things that didn't matter. They were just exchanging conversation and without the kids, they could lavish within their time together. When you're a parent, you rarely get the time to truly enjoy your spouse because the kids were always around. It was as if the kids had "parent quality time" radar.

You and your spouse could be on the couch enjoying a TV show, a movie, or just sitting there conversing back and forth, and your children would come and make it their business to interrupt you one way or another. Being a parent is a beautiful thing if you truly loved your kids. You may have your ups and downs but all and all, there's no greater feeling.

When they walked inside, they were met at the door by a waitress who asked them how many seats that they would need. After telling her just two, they were seated in a booth that gave them move privacy than being at the bar.

Dragonfly was an extremely nice, clean, and classy restaurant considering that it wasn't a best location. It wasn't a five star location either. A waitress walked over and asked them if they if they were ready to order. When they told her no, she asked if they wanted anything to drink. Tah ordered a double shot of Hennessy and Liz ordered an apple Margarita. They looked so good as a couple, the waitress didn't even bother to asked the two minors for their I.D.s.

Once she walked away, Tah pulled his phone out and turned the volume down, putting it on vibrate. Liz pulled out her phone to check in with Tahiry to see how the girls were doing. She'd told Liz that the babies were fine and not to text or call her again.

When Liz hung up, she quickly jumped on Facebook before Tah could say something to her. As soon as she logged onto her page, she saw back to back to pictures of Tahiry, Mya, and Malani on her news feed. Tahiry was social media crazy when she had her nieces with her. Liz liked each picture, then shared them with Tah on his page before logging out. By that time, their drinks had arrived. The waitress then asked if they were ready to order yet. Tah looked at Liz and asked her if she was ready to order. She grabbed the menu and asked the waitress to give them a little more time.

"No problem. Y'all take y'all time, okay?" the young waitress said, slightly giving Liz a flirtatious glimpse through the corner of her eye.

"Thank you," Tah replied, catching the look she gave her. He smiled and told Liz, "Ole girl look like she wanna get your pussy."

"Shut up, stupid!" Liz shot back, frowning her face up at Tah.

"I'm just saying."

"Well, don't just say. You know I ain't with that gay shit."

"You might not be, but she is and she definitely was just checking you out." Tah laughed, before taking a sip from his glass.

"Yeah, well she could forget it and if you was thinking about maybe getting a threesome popping off, then you could forget that too!" Liz said, giving him a funny look before her phone began to ring. He gave her a look that said "don't answer it" but when she saw that it was Tabi, she quickly picked up. "What's up, Tee?"

"Where are you at?"

"I'm out with my husband. Why, what's up?"

"Some mu'fucka's came through here asking questions about where Jerm got his shit from, so he told them none of their business," Tabi replied, sitting at her kitchen table smoking a blunt of sour diesel.

"That's what he was supposed to do," Liz said, cutting her off.

"Yeah, but check this out. They pulled off and came back around shooting."

"What?"

"What happened?" Tah asked, staring at his woman after hearing the concern in her voice.

"Yeah, wasn't nobody hit, but I just wanted you to know because Jerm is down there going crazy," Tabi said.

"He should be. Where was Doug at?" Liz asked, holding her right index finger up to Tah.

"Doug almost got hit. She's out trying to find GK so he could get the homies to go out looking for them niggas."

"She knows who it was?"

"Nah, she just feels some type of way and want GK and them to mob out looking for the car they were driving."

"Elizabeth, what happened?" Tah questioned more demandingly.

"Tell her to chill out. We don't need the Mafia homies in our business. I'll be over there when I leave here."

"A'ight."

"Yo, you don't fuck'n hear me talking to you!" Tah snapped, trying not to get upset.

Stuffing her phone back into her bag, Liz replied, "Sorry, bae. That was Tabi. She was telling me that some niggas came through Chadwick asking about the work the Jerm had. When he told them none of their business, they pulled off and came back shooting."

"Did anybody get hit?"

"No, but Doug's out there tryna get GK to round up the homies to ride around looking for somebody that she don't even know."

"What the fuck the nigga ask?" Tah asked as this piece of information grabbed his attention.

"I don't know. She didn't say, but that shit don't even matter."

"Yeah, you right."

CHAPTER 14
Friday
August 15, 2014
3:37 p.m. In Newark

"It seems like that shit is being spread out all over the city. Everywhere I turn around, mu'fuckas is popping up with this dope stamped Do Not Enter and Made In China," Pont said, sitting to Soo's left. They were in the backseat of Soo's pitch black Chevrolet Trailblazer which was parked on Central Avenue and 9th Street.

"That means that the mu'fucka that robbed us is out here somewhere selling that shit wholesale," Soo replied, nodding his head slowly as his son sat in the front seat watching *La Bamba*, a movie about Ritchie Valens. "He's tryna get rid of it before I can track him down. We gotta find these mu'fucka's before the family or Jahad gets wind of our lack of efforts. I need everything to stay casual until I finish setting things up. This shit can't fail."

"Jahad knows already. I talked to Cape the other day. He said that Jahad was pissed but said he was giving you the benefit of the doubt."

"Shit, we gotta do more than what we're doing. It's good you're out there putting it down, so at least he knows our presence is in the streets. But we need the niggas responsible for this shit and we need them quick."

"I feel you."

"And find out who the fuck is giving Jahad information behind my back."

"I'm on that already 'cause I figured you didn't know anything about that," Pont said as a red Suburban pulled up beside them.

"Who the fuck is this?" Pont asked, pulling out his .38 snub nose and cocking the hammer back. Tupac's "Hail Mary" was booming from the Suburban with a thunderous bass.

"Relax, that's my little bruh, Tarin. I told him to meet me here," Soo advised, stopping Pont before he did something that would make their situation even worse.

Soo knew Tarin rode around with goons with him that were always strapped down to the point of no return. Tarin had a lot to lose, so he kept a car full of Bloods with him. Not just that, Tarin tried to make sure that he had one or two cars filled with homies behind or in front of him. He wasn't taking any chances in the streets that had claimed so many lives before him.

When the back window of the Suburban came rolling down, Soo saw Tarin sitting there, wearing a white Paul George Indiana Pacers number 13 jersey with the blue and yellow stripes going down the sides. He had his two youngest sons in the car with him sitting there watching "Tom and Jerry" on the flat screen TV that hung from the roof of the Suburban. Behind them in the third row, was two homies strapped with P-90 rugers with extended clips.

"What's going on, Tarin? I almost thought you wasn't goin' come." Soo said, looking around to see how many cars Tarin had with him.

"Nah, I had to pick my boys up from their mother's house. You know how that goes."

"Yeah, I went through that this morning."

"What's up though? You got that for me?" Tarin asked, getting right down to business.

"Yeah, but the numbers went up a little bit because of thi—"

"Hold up. Wait, you gotta be kidding me. I'm not the nigga to pull this on. Soo, my money is always right and I always go hard," he replied, cutting Soo off before he could finish his statement.

"Yeah, you right. A'ight, look. Have your people meet my people in about ten minutes. You want the same order, right?"

"Nah, double that shit. You out here wild'n and shit, tryna over charge me. Let me get a bigger order just in case you run into some problems again."

"A'ight, I'm gonna need another ten minutes to get it there, so make that twenty minutes tops."

"It don't matter. I got somebody over there already with all of the bread. Just make sure that your people be there," Tarin said, before rolling his window back up and telling his driver to pull off.

"You must really fuck with that nigga 'cause you charging everybody else more no matter what they buying," Pont said as the Suburban pulled off just as easy as it pulled up.

"Yeah, he just put in an order for a whole brick of dope. He usually gets 500 grams but now he wants a whole thing. I need that money," Soo replied as a Newark Police cruiser pulled up right where Tarin's Suburban was double-parked.

"Makes sense then."

"Rasool, what's going on, friend?" the cop in the passenger seat greeted him after rolling his window down.

"Here, take that and keep it moving!" Pont replied for Soo, tossing $20,000 wrapped up in a brown paper bag into the police car.

"Thank you. Good doing business with you." The cop laughed, before pulling off.

"I can't stand them mu'fucka's!" Pont said, looking at the back window of the police cruiser.

"Yeah, me either, but they do what's needed of them," Soo told his little man.

* * *

4:49 p.m. In Roselle

"Tahiem, who are we inviting over for Thanksgiving dinner?" Liz asked, sitting on the edge of their California king size bed, getting dressed. Tah sat on the toilet in their master bathroom shitting with door open.

"There ain't going to no damn Thanksgiving in this house. You better take your ass over to Mattie's house with all of that Christian shit!" Tah told her, while reading *They Came Before Columbus* written by Ivan Van Sertima.

"Why do you have to be so fuck'n aggressive and nasty about it, though?"

"Because one, you know me better than that to think that I would be celebrating Thanksgiving, and two, there ain't shit to be thankful for on that day. The government uses that day to a cover up the way they murdered the Native Americans."

"That's not what they taught us in school. The Pilgrims and the Indians were feasting out of friendship," Liz told Tah as Travis walked into the room, bringing back Tah's wireless XBox controller.

"Well, the Iman gave me some food for thought on the whole Thanksgiving scam," Tah said, wiping his ass using his left hand, then flushing the toilet. "The truth behind the whole extortion of the holiday is the Pilgrims weren't looking for religious freedom as they say. They were looking to take over new land. In 1614, an English soldier named John Smith came to the East Coast. He started selling Pawtuxet Native Americans to the Europeans, giving the Pawtuxet blankets that were infected with smallpox."

"Smallpox?" Liz and Travis asked, hanging on to Tah's every word. He grabbed his washcloth, lathered it up with soap, and began to wipe in between his ass cheeks.

"Yeah, smallpox. The Native Americans didn't know anything about the disease, and they didn't have the cure for it. So, while John Smith was going around kidnapping, other Europeans were here spreading smallpox, killing the rest of the Pawtuxet villages.

By the year 1620, after Pilgrims got here, the Pawtuxet was no more. So the Pilgrims built a colony and named it The Plymouth Plantation," he continued, scrubbing his ass with his soapy rag, making sure to clean himself as best as he could. "One member of the Pawtuxet named, Squanto, survived. Then he turned around and taught the Pilgrims how to farm and fish. He also taught them about herbs and fruit. Without his help, the Plymouth Plantation wouldn't have survived the first winter."

"So, what do that have to do with Thanksgiving? All you stated was how the white people took land from the Indians," Liz said just as Tah was ringing out his rag.

"If you let me finish, I'll teach y'all lil' asses something! The Pilgrims began to call themselves Puritans and with the help from Squanto, they befriended the Wampanaog nation. At the end of the first year, the Puritans had a feast that didn't include the Native Americans. The feast took place in 1629 and the following three days after the feast, was their thanksgiving. They celebrated the fortune they made off of the Pawtuxet. They sodomized the Native American women and forced violence upon the rest, killing the chief of the Wampanoag. They hung his head on a pole in Plymouth, Massachusetts where it stayed for twenty-four years."

"Damn!" Travis said, shaking his head as he walked back out of Tah's room with his rack of Muslim oils.

"I never knew that," Liz said, tears welling in her eyes as she stood in front of her vanity, holding her keys in her left hand.

"*Assassinations, diplomatic relations killed indigenous people, built a new nation,*" Tah rapped, sounding almost like Nas did on "America", pulling his pants up. "Anyway, where are you and Tahi going tonight?"

"I don't know. She's talking about going to Club Onyx with Tabi."

"In Philly?"

"Yeah."

"You be careful. Philly ain't no joke. Shit gets real out there in two point five."

"I know. Stop at the bank and put some more money in my checking account, I love you," Liz replied, before dashing out of the room, leaving Tah to his own thoughts.

Tah stood in his bedroom wearing a pair of Evisu jeans, a white Miskeen long sleeve shirt, and a pair of grey, blue, and orange Elite Edition New Balance 574's as he prepared to leave his house, as well. Tammy had the girls for the weekend. She said that she missed them, so this was Tah's time to enjoy being free again without having to worry about calling anybody. He'd taken his G.E.D. online yesterday because he knew he wouldn't have the time to go to school. His plans to get rid of his drugs needed him in the streets full-time.

Tah stuffed his black leather Polo wallet with $2,000, then left out of the room to go meet up with Phenom. Travis met Tah at the front door with his PSP in his hands, looking up at his brother. Tah came down the stairs with his navy blue butter soft JCME leather jacket on. When they walked outside, they saw Liz climbing into Tahiry's Lacrosse.

Tahiry was at the salon getting her hair done, so she was driving her car. James Robbin and Phenom were in the new precinct on Bergen Street and Clinton Avenue, talking to homicide in reference to clearing his name. Tah told Champ to bring Maar and Benny up north so they could have a sit down, telling Phenom the same thing with Bino and his crew. Tah had Tahiry call Havok about entertainment for the meeting. He wanted to make sure everybody was comfortable before the meeting.

Travis and Tah hopped into the Tahoe and drove out of Roselle headed to Newark. He had a meeting with Big Ant, the big homie that ran Madison Avenue. Tah wanted to rent some space for Doc and Phantom, not wanting Big Ant to feel like he was just moving in on his shit, even though Tah had been living around there for a while.

Tah was well aware of all of the things that were kicking off inside his circle. The only thing he wasn't aware of was that Dez was in Trenton killing Raye's boys. The whole time Tah was driving, he never noticed the Volvo S60 that was three cars behind him. It was the same S60 that was sitting outside of the courthouse three days ago, taking pictures. They'd been watching him since the day Doc started hustling on Madison Avenue, the moment that they took the drugs from the house on 11th Street.

* * *

Meanwhile in Newark

"Mr. Dickens, can you please explain how your fingerprints managed to get on the bullet that was lodged in our murdered victim?" Detective Maur asked, sitting across the table from James Robbin and Phenom.

"I got this," James Robbin said, putting his right hand on Phenom's left shoulder. "My client pleads the fifth on that question to keep from incriminating himself or bringing harm to his family."

"We can respect that but we're going to need something to get a proper understanding as to why we shouldn't charge him with this crime," Sgt. Wright returned, staring at Phenom as he tried to avoid eye contact with James Robbin.

James Robbin leaned over and whispered into Phenom's ear. He turned around and leaned back into his ear, then said, "All we can give you is him admitting to touching the bullet before it was placed into whatever gun it was fired from. He doesn't own a gun nor has used a gun in any threatening manner."

"I don't believe you! Prove it!" Detective Maur snapped, trying to pin Phenom in a corner.

"Prove it how?" Phenom asked, finally allowing his voice to be heard.

"Take a lie detector test."

"We don't have a problem with taking a lie detector test, but first I want you to show me a gun, and a statement from a witness putting my client behind the gun. Just give me a solid, concrete, and slam dunk reason to even think about having my client take a lie detector test," James Robbin shot back, hitting them where he knew it would hurt. "You're asking a lot from a man who's only here to answer a few questions about a crime where his close friend is still in a hospital deep in a coma, hanging on to her life."

"Is that motive you just gave us?" Detective Maur asked, trying to hide the hint of a smile.

"I dare you to use it as motive and I'll have you and your partner working traffic before the ink could dry on your paperwork!" James Robbin snapped, looking from Detective Maur to Sgt. Wright as he gave them a serious, uncomfortable stare.

Phenom was smiling on the inside even though he was sitting there with a deadly cold expression upon his face. He wanted to burst out into a ball of laughter at the way James Robbin had the two detectives by their balls. He had never seen a lawyer go hard the way he was going hard for him, and he didn't even know him.

However, he was determined to prove he hadn't committed the murder he did in fact commit. On top of the money that Tah had given James Robbin, Phenom had given him another $4,000 today when they met up at the precinct. He was beyond impressed with his work ethic and would pay him whatever he wanted because he was that convinced.

James Robbin had let it be known before they even walked into the building that they were only there to answer a few questions and once they were done, Phenom was walking right out of the precinct with him, no questions asked! The homie Tarin had definitely come through for them with this one. James Robbin was everything that a gangster needed when taking steps into the criminal world.

"How could you sleep at night knowing that you defend murderers?" Detective Maur questioned.

"Since you're asking me about how I sleep at night, I take it that we are done here with the questioning," James Robbin said, collecting the papers that he had laid across the table.

"We're done here for now, but make sure that your client doesn't go far."

"Now why would I stop a free man from going where he wants to go? If you have any more questions, you can contact my office, but I strongly suggest that you leave my client alone," he replied, staring down at the detectives as if they were his children. "This here is a innocent man and I expect for him to be treated as one."

"Well, that's good that you expect that because that's far from what he's gonna get," Detective Maur shot back, caring less and less about how James Robbin felt about how he did his job. "I'm going to keep looking into this. I just don't believe that Mr. Dickens is this saint that you're making him out to be!"

"I suggest that you watch yourself and the thin—"

"Fuck your suggestions!" he barked, startling James Robbin while making Phenom tense up ready to attack. "You don't come in here telling me and my partner what the fuck we can and can't do!"

"Maur, calm down," Sgt. Wright told his partner as Lt. Microsoft walked into interrogation room 3.

"I don't know who the fuc—" James Robbin began before he was cut off.

"Enough! Mr. Robbin, you and your client can go now. If we have any other questions, we'll contact your office," Lt. Microsoft said, standing in the doorway.

"I bet you will!" James Robbin replied, standing up and leading the way out of the room.

"Don't go too far, Dickens. This isn't over," Detective Maur told Phenom before James Robbin could walk out of the room.

"Was that a threat?" James Robbin turned around and asked, standing in front of Lt. Microsoft.

"No, that was a promise. This is only the beginning."

"I said enough. You say another word and I'll suspend your ass without pay!" Lt. Microsoft barked, shooting Detective Maur one of the coldest stares. "Mr. Robbin, you may leave."

"We're leaving, but believe me and you, this won't end right here!"

CHAPTER 15
Friday
August 29, 2014
That Night in Newark

"When did you get back from Trenton?" Tammy asked as Tah walked into the apartment.

"I'm not here right now. You don't see me," he replied, heading straight towards his room to grab the money he had put there last week.

"If I don't see you, then I must be drunker than I thought!"

"Yeah, that's it. You're drunker than you thought. Now, can you leave me alone? I'm tryna do something."

"Nigga, this is my shit! You don't live here no more!" Tammy shot back, storming towards Tah's room.

"I don't live here anymore, but I pay the bills in here. Don't ever forget that."

"I don't give a fuck what you pay. You don't live up in this mu'fucka, so don't get cocky with me, you lil' shit!"

Tah stood up with the bookbag filled with money. He felt the urge to move it for some reason or another. He had just gotten back into town after going down to Millville and Trenton to meet the out-of-town help. As soon as he reached Newark, he felt he should move his money. Phenom and Champ were still in southern New Jersey, but Tah couldn't stay away for too long.

Phenom left Phantom and Known up north with Tah to watch his back while he was away. They were trained to go at any moment. Tah liked how they handled business. He never had to tell them when to pull their guns or when to let them off.

"What is that?"

"None of your business. You gon' learn to mind your business sometimes, old lady," Tah told her and laughed, tossing the bookbag over his shoulder.

"Old?"

"Aye, if the shoe fits wear it."

"I can't stand your ass!" Tammy snapped as he walked past her still laughing. "Your ugly ass!"

"It takes one to know one."

"Your father called yesterday looking for you."

"Let him keep calling. I don't know why you even accept his calls. You're wasting your time with that nigga."

"You need to talk to your father, Taheim."

"Yeah, yeah, yeah. Don't forget that you got Travis this weekend," Tah replied, walking out of the apartment.

Tah walked downstairs thinking about his next move, things down south are really moving so he had some things he wanted to do. He walked out onto Madison and looked in every direction as he made his way to his truck, with *37,000 hanging on his back. A Volvo S60 sat up the street watching Tah's every move, and as he climbed into his car and pulled off, they were right behind him. Even if Tah was on point he wouldn't have seen them coming, the Volvo was a car everybody looked past.

* * *

In Roselle

"How much did you come up with over there?" Liz asked Tahiry as they sat in her living room with a table full of money.

"I counted $113,700."

"Okay, that's what I counted before I counted this $38,000 right here. I can't even begin to imagine where Tahiem got this money from. This is a lot of fuck'n money!" she said nervously, shaking her head.

"I couldn't tell you," Tahiry lied, refusing to look Liz in the face. Tah made her promise to never confide in Liz about his business. "He dropped it off to me and told me to have you help me count it, so that's what I did."

"I hope he ain't do nothing that will put us in danger."

"Nah, Tah's too smart for that."

"I pray you're right because this money combined with the money he was throwing around is really starting to scare me. I can't lose him like I did Roc," Liz admitted, getting teary-eyed.

I know I might sound crazy
But after all that I still love you
You wanna come back in my life
Now there's something that I have to do
I have to tell the ones that I can't adore
That they can't have my love no more

"Thank you, God!" Tahiry said to herself as Amanda Perez's "Angel" ringtone started playing, alerting her that Tah was calling.

Tah had not only held a meeting with Big Ant, he sold him two kilos of dope at $69 a gram, knowing everybody else was charging $85 to $95 a gram. Because Tah agreed to sell him work at low prices, Big Ant agreed to let Tah move work on the block rent free. Doc and Phantom already had their own clientele, so they weren't worried about nothing. Tah paid Tahiry another $10,000 just to pick the money up from Big Ant's little brother and drop off the keys. It was the easiest money that she had ever made.

Tahiry had been told about the meeting and the party, but she chose not to go. She knew Tah was going to be there. She didn't want to be around him when he started fucking with around with other bitches. Tah wasn't sure if he wanted to settle down with one female, but Tahiry made it clear that she was a one-man woman. She knew she was starting to catch feelings, a little upset he chose to go to the strip club instead of hanging out with her.

"Hello," Liz greeted, putting her phone on speaker and sitting it on the table.

"As salaamu alaikum," Tah returned, climbing into his Tahoe and closing the door.

"Wa alaikum salaam. What are you doing, bae?"

"I'm leaving the Mansion right now. I'm on my way home," he told her as he pulled away from the curb, noticing the Volvo S60 for the first time. "What are you wearing?"

"Ummmm, ill!" Tahiry gasped, pretending to gag on her left index finger.

"Knock it off. I never once pegged you to be such a hater."

"My girl ain't no hater. Your ass need to stop being so damn nasty all of the fuck'n time," Liz told him, blushing.

"Man, fuck all of that. Tahi knows how we get down, so she better get with the program," Tah said, heading up to St. George Avenue still watching his mirrors for the Volvo S60.

"Did you talk to your mother?" Liz asked, tossing Tahiry a bag of sour diesel to roll up.

"Nah. She got the girls, right?"

"No, she dropped them off early talking about they broke the wire to her TV. She said they couldn't stay the night because they were bad as hell."

"Fuck outta here, I paid her ass a hundred dollars to watch them overnight!" Tah snapped, making a right on to McCarter Highway.

"Yeah, well she came and dropped them off and ain't give me no money back."

"I hope she don't spend it all in one place 'cause her ass won't be getting no more money from me for a very long fuck'n time!" he shot back, switching lanes as he played his mirrors. "Tahiry you better get your mu'fuck'n godmother before I do something to her."

"Whatever, nigga. Just hurry your ass up so I can go home already," Tahiry told him, splitting the vanilla dutch down the middle after breaking the weed up. Liz was stuffing money inside of a black JCME suitcase which sat on the floor in front of the table.

"Yeah, a'ight," he shot back, pausing to look in his mirror to see where the Volvo S60 was at. "We all know your ass is about to text Doc for the address so you can pop in on niggas."

"Ain't nobody even thinking about y'all lil' dirty asses. How you know I'm not meeting up with another nigga?"

"'Cause you ain't 'bout that life."

"Fuck outta here. I'll show you who 'bout that life!" Tahiry spat, getting mad as she watched Liz double over in laughter on the couch.

"Show me, make your brother a believer. Better yet, make yourself a believer." He laughed, picking up speed as he saw the Volvo S60 switch lanes behind him. He was attempting to lose his tail.

"You know what? Fuck you and your fake ass wife. My pain isn't some damn comedy special!"

"Okay, okay, okay. That's enough," Liz told them both, still laughing. She was trying to stop herself from laughing even harder. "Bae, leave my sister alone before we jump you."

"He better act like he know."

"Hold up," Liz said, realizing she couldn't hear Tah's radio in the background anymore. "Hello?

"I know this nigga ain't hang up on you," Tahiry said as Liz looked at her phone confused.

"Hello? Tah, hello?"

* * *

Back in Newark

"What time are you coming home, Greg?"

"Whatever mu'fuckn time I feel like it! Stop questioning me all the time! I keep telling you about yourself," Phenom snapped, grabbing his keys on his way to the door.

"I don't know who you think you be talking to, but I'm not scared of your ass!" Stacie shot back, following him closely.

"Yeah, a'ight. If you leave the house, make sure you close the windows."

"Kiss my ass, nigga!"

"Later, I got things to do right now," he replied, walking out of the door.

"Don't be surprised if your shit is on the sidewalk when you come back."

"You know better. Now go inside with all of that noise. I love you," Phenom said, nearing his car.

"Love you, too."

Just like that, Phenom was in the car and Stacie was back in the house going on about her business. He was on his way to see Phantom and Known before he met up with Tah. The two of them had just come from Trenton a few hours ago. Phenom barely had any time to rest before he was right back at it. He had to flood Trenton while he had the chance. He knew with the right crew, he could flip the town.

By the time he was on Fairmont Avenue and 15th Avenue, he found himself boxed in by three other cars. He quickly grabbed his gun and lowered his window. Before anyone could get out of their cars, Phenom starting letting those rounds off. Bullets tore through the windshield of the car directly in front of his, tearing into the chest of the passenger.

He stood up and turned his aim towards the car to his left, the driver backing up as shots came from the third car which backed up, too. A bullet bounced off of the roof of his car, just missing his right shoulder. Phenom wasn't the least bit fazed by the bullets flying past him.

All three cars quickly backed up just as fast as they had swarmed in. Phenom was now in the middle of the street, sending shots after the cars. Eleven shots went by so fast, pissed him off even more. He didn't know who was in those cars, but he did know they weren't boxing him in to ask for directions. He ran back to his car and hopped in with hopes of catching up with one of them.

* * *

"Tahiry, what the fuck?" Liz screamed, trembling nervously as she paced back and forth in the living room. Tahiry sat on the beige leather loveseat watching Liz with concern in her eyes. "I've been calling Tahiem's phone for over an hour. Where the fuck is my husband at?"

"Liz, just calm down. Let's not jump to conclusions. For all we know, his phone could've died," Tahiry replied, silently praying that Tah was okay.

"I'm not jumping to anything! I'm going off of what the fuck I got!"

"Baby girl, I'm just as concerned about Tah as you are, but we gotta stay focused just in case we have to deal with the worse. We can't be off balance."

Liz stopped pacing long enough to look her. That's when she saw Tahiry was just as worried as she was. She actually looked like she had aged a few years from the stressed expression on her face. Tah was Liz's everything besides Mya and Malani. Her heart was badly hurting because she couldn't reach him. It wasn't like him to not contact her, somehow knowing she would be worried.

Tahiry couldn't take it any longer, so she hopped up and rushed to Liz's side, wrapping her arms around her sister. She knew they both needed some comforting right now. Tah meant a lot to both of them and if something had happened to him, they both would be extremely hurt. That would too much to come back from.

Holding Liz in her arms let her truly know just how scared Liz as they both were shaking horribly. They both were breaking down. Tahiry could only say another silent prayer, hoping Tah was okay. She needed her brother to call them and so they would know he was okay.

"Tahi, where could he be?" Liz asked as all of her emotions spilled over, pulling a wagon of tears down her cheeks.

Tahiry started crying even harder. "I don't know, baby girl. I just don't."

* * *

3:33 p.m. In Wildwood, New Jersey

Dave M.: What's good?

Bob: I need to come see you real quick. You still got that same thing?

Dave M.: Yeah, I'm on Garfield but I'm about to go back to Roberts, so you better hurry up

Bob: No problem, bro. I'm on Oak right now, turning onto Hudson.

Dave M.: A'ight, meet me on the corner of Park

"Yo, nigga. You goin' pass the blunt or what?" Stallion asked, standing next to Dave M.'s white Cadillac CTS which was parked on the corner of Park Boulevard and W. Spicer Avenue.

"Man, who said that I was smoking with you, bruh?" Dave M. returned, lifting the blunt back to his lips before taking a pull of it.

Bob: A'ight, I'll be right there.

"Come on, bro. Don't fuck around. I ain't been standing here all of this time just cause I look good!"

"I know damn well that wasn't the case because you look like shit!" he snapped as his girlfriend, Sofi, rolled the passenger window down and handed him his other phone.

"It's your mother," Sofi told him, giving him a funny look that told him to read between the lines.

"You're the fuck'n worse!" Stallion told Dave M., while walking off towards W. Lincoln Avenue headed to the Sandman Towers. "I'ma just go get a bag from Skinny Man. I hope you choke off that shit!"

"I know, I know. We wish we could get the best things that life has to offer. Unfortunately, it don't work like that, buddy." Dave M. laughed, watching Stallion walk away as a tan Honda Accord ES pulled up on W. Garfield Avenue.

You ain't no friend of mine (bitch)
You ain't kin of mine
What makes you think that I won't run up on you with the
nine
We do this every time
Right now we on the grind
So hurry up and cop and go
We selling nicks and dimes
Shorty she so fine I gotta make her mine
An ass like that gotta be one of a kind

"Hello?" Dave M. greeted, pressing the phone that Sofi handed him. He was also checking the text message he got from his trap phone the 50 Cent "Wanksta" ringtone alerted him of.

"What's good, white boy. Where you at?" Tah asked him. "I'm in a hood near you."

"Who the fuck is this?" he shot back, removing his phone from his ear to look at the name.

"It damn sure ain't your old ass momma, nigga!"

"Fuck you, Tah. W hat the fuck you doing down here where you can't go no further?"

Bob: I'm here. Where are you?

"I came to see my favorite white boy. You still over there on the boardwalk?"

"Nah, I'm about to have my girl text you the address."

"A'ight, hurry up 'cause I think I might be lost."

Dave M.: I'm coming out now. Just park on the corner.

"Baby, text Tah the address to my apartment. I'm about to go meet Bob," Dave M. told her, handing her the phone back.

Bob: A'ight, bet.

Lincoln Dave Meyers was born in Wildwood, New Jersey where he grew up watching some of the best do what they do. Dave M. was a 25-year old street hustler. He was just as ruthless as any of the African Americans in his neighborhood. He had his own little hustle going on down there even though Skinny Man ran the projects called Sandman Towers.

Sandman Towers was located on W. Lincoln Avenue and whatever you might need could be found there. Tah and Dave M. had met while Tah, Tahiry, Mattie, and Liz were down there two years before for Tahiry's birthday. Because they didn't have the kids with them, Tah was trying to turn up.

Looking for some good weed down there, he ended up on W. Roberts Avenue. Tah spoke to Dave M. about buying an ounce of weed and the next thing you know, they were all up inside of a local club! Dave M. had not only taken them to get some weed, but he ended up taking them to Flip Flops on 4th Street.

The five of them partied so hard, they all woke up in still drunk and high out of their minds. Mattie had stayed in their room and had hooked up with a guy she had met at the Hurricanes Topless Bar on Pacific Avenue and E. Schelienger Avenue. That's really what she needed more than anything.

They had partied like fucking rock stars that entire weekend. One would've thought that they had known each other for decades. Dave M. and Tah clicked so well, they exchanged numbers and had stayed in contact with each other.

Over the years, Dave M. had even come up to Newark a few times to chill with Tah and Chadwick Girlz. Tah knew that he was down at the bottom doing his thing. He just didn't know how much, but he knew Dave M. could use the prices and work that he had.

Dave M. served Bob, then walked back to his CTS and climbed in. He knew if Tah called him, he wasn't far away, so he wanted to hurry up and get to his house. Tah never just popped up, so he knew that something was up, and frankly, he wanted to know what it was. Tah hadn't called him and said anything, wanting to talk in person. He was hell bent not talking business at all on his phone.

Dave M. got into his CTS and pulled off, making a right onto W. Spicer Avenue. He was listening to Tupac's "Until The End Of Time" smoking a cigarette. When he reached Susquehanna Avenue, he made a left and drove down to W. Roberts Avenue. As soon as he made the left onto W. Roberts Avenue, he spotted Tah climbing out of his Tahoe that was parked right in front of his apartment.

Tah climbed out of his SUV with Phenom, Phantom, and Phantom's little brother, Known. All three of them were armed with black chrome .45 desert eagles. They all canvassed the area knowing they could easily get left in Wildwood in a blink of an eye. You may know Wildwood for the boardwalk and rides, but evil also lied in between all of that tourist shit.

"Tah, what's good nigga? What the fuck you doing down here in my hood unannounced?" Dave M. questioned, making sure he grabbed his 9-millimeter before climbing out of his CTS.

"I had to come down here and talk some business with my nigga."

"Business?"

"Yeah, nigga, business. I know you down here moving things. I figured I'd come spread some love," Tah said, eyeing Sofi down as she climbed out of the Cadillac looking just like a blonde haired Ashley Graham in her dark blue, coochie cutting Levi denim jean shorts and pink True Religion tank top.

"What type of love you tryna spread?"

"Damn, she bad than a mu'fucka!" KnowN mumbled, staring at Sofi hard as hell.

"I know, that's why I'm with her!" Dave M. replied, letting Known know he heard him.

"Yo, my bad, bruh. I was jus—"

"Don't worry about it. The bitch is bad. I can't fault you for speaking facts."

"Yo, you stole with her, dead ass!" Phenom told him, as Sofi walked up and hugged Dave M. from behind.

"Thank you," she replied, blushing as she squeezed him tighter.

"Look, I got prices that you ain't goin' get nowhere else," Tah told him, looking around as a few females walked by across the street in their bikinis and stilettos.

"Prices?"

"Yeah, I got them shit's for the low low."

"Since when did you become the plug?" Dave M. asked, looking at Tah with a puzzled expression on his face.

"Does it really even matter?" Sofi shot back, looking at her man like he lost his mind. "A plug is a plug and if he got prices that Skinny Man can't beat, then we making the move!"

"Slow down, baby girl. Grown folks is talking."

"Look, I got everything you can need and I'm sliding them to you at the lowest rate possible in the streets," Tah told him as another chick walked by giving Tah and Phantom lustful stares.

"A'ight, where the samples? I can't just jump off of the deep end without sampling the product first," Dave M. said, still shocked that Tah was dealing with drugs after everything that he told him about his father.

"Known, go grab that for him."

"And you came prepared?" Sofi gasped, looking at Dave M. She was trying to persuade him to fuck with Tah. "I like your style, Tahiem!"

"A'ight, a'ight. Settle down, baby girl. Let's see if the fish is fresh before we go jumping into the ocean with no life jackets."

"Trust me, this shit is going to take Wildwood by storm!" Tah said, smiling at how good he knew that his product was.

Duquie Wilson

CHAPTER 16
Thursday
September 11, 2014
9:27 p.m. In Trenton

"Damn, them niggas is eating down there. Raye gon' have to do something 'cause his little scare tactics ain't working," the tall kid sitting at the table said, rolling a blunt of sour diesel. "We losing more niggas by the day, while their still bringing in money by the boatload!"

"Don't worry about it. My brother got something real nice setup for a bitch. We going to nef house and kidnap his family," Todd replied, taking a sip of his peach E&J Brandy. "A bitch ain't gon' know where it came from. Nef don't even know we'vd been following him home every night."

"Oh, a'ight. That's what the fuck I'm talking about."

"Yeah, nef just sitting back thinking that a bitch just letting shit slide right now. My brother ain't forget shit!"

"Word, nef definitely know that Bino was behind a bitch getting shot last month," the other kid jumped in, remembering going to the hospital for a bullet wound to his right leg.

"Nah, a bitch been letting the heat die down, but I've been telling Raye that it's time to make a move on Bino and Rah. But like always, he keeps telling me to chill."

"Yeah, well I talked to Drip and he said Bino ain't the one putting it down," the tall kid said. "He said it's some O.T. niggas out here putting on for the nigga Bino."

"And how would Drip know anything?" Todd asked, mad that he was always the last to find out about things.

"He running with them now. Bitch called himself rubbing it in my face when he was telling me."

"Todd, bring me that bag off of the couch so I can put that money up," the tall kid called out, ready to get up out of the house so he could go meet up with his shorty.

"Nah, we gotta make sure that every single dollar is wrapped up and accounted for," Todd told him.

"We did that shit already. You just tryna sit up in here so you won't get caught slipping again," the other kid announced. "You think I ain't notice, but a bitch ain't stupid. Every night around this time, you wanna stay cooped up in the hut until ten o'clock!"

"Fuck you, nigga. I'll go outside at any time! I don't give fuck who out there!" Todd barked angrily, looking at the kid like he had lost his mind.

Outside parked in a white Honda Civic rental, Dez and Temp were canvassing the block. Raye's new stash house on located on Greenwood Avenue and Walnut Avenue, many blocks away from South Walter Avenue assessing everything.

Rah was in the backseat caressing his AR-15, anticipating the move he had been craving for since Halloween night. He still hadn't gotten over Glee's death. Though Glee only rolled with them for a few weeks, he had known him nearly all of his young life. Glee was a good nigga and Rah had taken a liking to him. So each and every time he killed one of Raye's homies, he chalked that up as another win for Glee. He wasn't going to be happy until Raye was face down in the gutter where he felt he belonged.

* * *

Saturday
September 20, 2014
8:39 p.m. In Newark On Madison Street

"Feds!" Champ exclaimed, sitting in the passenger seat of Tah's Tahoe as they sat parked across the street from Tammy's house.

"Yeah, I think they followed me from the house that night," Tah said, looking out of the window to his right. "I'm almost sure that it was them."

"Why are now you just saying something about it?" Phenom questioned him, sitting to Tah's left.

"Because today is the first day I haven't seen them following me. Got me feeling like I'm fuck'n John Gotti or somebody!"

"Really, Tah," Champ laughed, looking at him through the rearview mirror as 2 fiends walked up on Doug and Vee. "Of all of the people you could feel like, you feel like John Gotti?"

"Yeah, mu'fucka. That car has been following me for over a month now. That's just the about the same time when I first saw it," Tah shot back, rubbing his temples. "I need y'all to be alert more than ever now. We got death penalties sitting in Kearny."

"Have you ever stopped to think that maybe the feds have been following you since Mujid got cuffed?" Champ asked, looking over at Doug serve the fiends.

"Could've, but I don't know for sure, so just keep your eyes open at all times. Circle the block before you park and really watch what you say over the phone."

"A'ight."

"Doc is already in route to you, so everything will be there once you get down there."

"A'ight and Tahiry should be texting you to let you know she received the bread."

"How much is it?" Phenom asked, knowing that Champ had been short the last time he came to pick up.

"Fifteen stacks. It's a lil short, but I got you on the next go around."

"Fuck you mean!" Phenom barked, watching another group of fiends approach Doug and Vee.

"Gee, chill. It's aight," Tah said, shaking his head at the fact that Champ was lacking.

"How the fuck is he down there running shit but his money keep coming up short?" he snapped, staring at the back of Champ's head with heated anger. "The third law set was that everybody's money be correct, no matter who the fuck you are!"

"I said it's a'ight," Tah growled as a white Dodge Challenger R/T drove by playing Jadakiss' "By Your Side".

"Good looking, Tah," Champ weakly returned, grabbing the door handle trying to make his escape.

> *You can have it your way*
> *How do you want it*
> *You goin' back that ass up*
> *Or should I push up on it*
> *Temperature rising okay*
> *Let's go to the next level*
> *Dance floor jam packed*
> *Hot as a tea kettle*

50 Cent's *"Candy Shop"* ringtone featuring Olivia sounded off as Champ climbed out of the Tahoe. As he quickly walked off, Phenom turned to Tah and said, "I think Champ's getting high, son!"

"Don't tell me you really think that Champ is getting high!" Tah said, looking at Phenom as if he had lost his ever loving mind.

"Yeah, why else do you think his money keep coming up short?"

"Damn, we ain't even been rolling that long and already you're tryna take Champ outta the circle!" he said, looking at his phone as he read the text Liz just sent him.

Liz: Hey. What's up, daddy?

"Everybody else is following the laws that you set. Why is it any different for Champ?" Phenom asked, watching Champ climbed into his Taurus as Tah texted Liz back.

"Maybe Champ's having problems down there in Millville. Have you thought about that before tagging him for getting high on his own shit?"

"You don't think he would've said something knowing that we got his back?"

"Well, do you got his back?" Tah asked, sending his message.

Tah: What's up, bae? What's the matter?

"What type of fuck'n question is that!" Phenom snapped, causing Phantom to look back at him.

"I'm saying, you ready to take him out cause he's struggling instead of living by the bro code and helping our brother."

> *You can have it your way*
> *how do you want it*
> *you goin' back that ass up or*
> *should I push up on it—*

As Tah opened the text message from Liz before the ringtone could finish, Phenom humbly replied, "You're right. I'ma call him later and have a talk to him."

"Now that sounds better," Tah replied, reading Liz's message as a red Ford Expedition pulled up in front of Doug and Vee.

Liz: Nothing. I just miss you, that's all. Where are you at? What are you doing? Who are you with? I'm bored.

Tah smiled to himself knowing that Liz was just worried about him more than being jealous. She wasn't about to lose him for anything. Since the night when he'd dropped his phone trying to get away from the Volvo S60 a few weeks ago, Liz has been a nervous wreck.

That night, Tah's 2S had fell between his legs and his screen cracked after sliding under the gas pedal. So every time that Liz called him, he couldn't answer. Then it just started sending her to voicemail. Since then, each time Tah left home now, she got extremely nervous. Then once Doc told the girls how Candy Girls was designed, she became even more jealous now that Tah and Phenom had been there four times since then.

After hearing about their night in Rahway, Tahiry cut Champ off as Liz started pressing Tah more about other women. Money was rolling in quickly and Liz was starting to see less and less of her man. Tah had to smile knowing how his baby was at home going through it right now.

He hadn't cheated on her and had no intentions of doing so, but it was flattering his woman got so jealous over him. Tah was texting Liz back as the fiends climbed back into the Expedition. He knew he loved his baby with all of his heart and would die showing her just how much.

Tah: I miss you too, bae. I'm out and about. Just as bored as you are

"Yo, Stacie has been down my back about moving in with her," Phenom said, looking at the Expedition that pulled off as Tabi and Jerm walked up on Doug and Vee.

"I don't know why you don't just go ahead and do it. You're there every fuck'n night anyway!" Tah laughed as his 2S started vibrating before The Game's "Hate It or Love It" sounded off.

"Nah, if I do that, she gon' think that she own me and shit."

"Nigga, she do own your ass!" he continued, laughing harder now than he was before, opening Tahiry's text message.

"Fuck you, nigga!" Phenom shot back just when a Chevrolet Lumina pulled up on Doug, Vee, Jerm, and Tabi.

Tahiry: Mommy just dropped off your lunch money. I keep telling you I'm not your piggy bank!

Doug and Doc had completely moved their entire operation up on Madison Avenue, cutting GK off completely. Tah was hitting them with unbelievable prices, so they were ready to move out on their own. Then to top everything off, Tah had talked to Big Ant. They decided to come together business wise, which opened up the trap even more for the girls. Now they were running Madison Avenue from 18th Street down to 17th Street.

Big Ant made it so that none of the homies sold on that one block. In return, Tah dropped the price for him a little bit more. Big Ant had also cut his connect off after getting the prices Tah was giving him. Tah was the link missing from his chain of operations. Things in Tah's reach were starting to pick up. The only thing that hadn't improved was China still being in a coma. She was missing all of this.

Tah: Whatever, put it up for me. I'll be there after work

As Tah was sending Tahiry a text, two men dressed in dark colors climbed out of the Lumina/ Phenom's antennas went flying to the roof as he reached for his .45 caliber. Since getting the arrest warrant lifted, the police somewhat back off of him thanks to James Robbin.

Phenom had been back home spending more time in Newark by Tah's side and with his boy Phantom who was now Tah's new driver. Since Tah didn't have his license yet, Tahiry, Liz, and Mattie agreed it was he got one. Phenom couldn't be the driver because he wanted to make sure he

191

remained alert and ready to shoot at all times. After all, he was the muscle.

Phenom backed up from the drugs and let his cousin Bino do his thing so he could focus on keeping Tah safe. Phenom just wanted to kill motherfuckers. So Tah was paying him to basically protect him and his investment around the clock, and making sure that Doc and Tabi were safe when they made their trips to Trenton, Millville, and Wildwood. Doug and the Chadwick Girlz were moving their work with ease, as well as work for Tah. It was a win-win for everybody because they were all making crazy money.

Now that Liz was a stay at home mother and wife, she'd taken a step back from the Chadwick Girlz. She was still calling shots, but she wasn't on the front line with them anymore. It was all good because Chela, Mona, and Lissa had finally came home today from the Youth House.

Thanks to Tah getting them a good lawyer, they all beat their charges with no questions asked. The three wildest and youngest of the bunch were anxious and excited to get home and indulge in the money their crew was getting. They'd been getting the money Tah had sent them, hearing how they were on the streets blowing money fast.

They weren't on the block right now because Tah gave them each $2,000 for a shopping spree, so they all went downtown to blow through each and every store.

Tah told them that he wanted to talk to them before he put anything in their hands. Plus, he wanted to find a spot just for them so they could spread their wings and grow as one outside of the Chadwick Girlz.

Tahiry was busy trying to finalize everything with Tah's tattoo shop and his laundromat. Her and Mattie were trying to make sure all of his paperwork was legit. Tabi and Doc had been extra busy driving drugs back and forth to Trenton,

Wildwood, and Millville a lot lately, so they really hadn't been around the crew as much, but Tah was paying them good money to make each trip.

"What the fuck!" Phenom barked, grabbing the door handle and shoving the door open, causing Tah to look up from his phone.

Tat, tat, tat, tat, tat, tat, tat, tat, tat, tat, tat, tat, tat, tat, tat!

"Shit!" Tah yelled, shoving his door open as he climbed out with his 9-millimeter in his right hand.

"Aaaahhhhhhhh!!!" the girls screamed as bullets from an AK-47 flew past their heads in all directions.

Bok! Bok! Bok! Bok!

Phenom walked down one of the shooters as they tried to make it back to the Lumina. They were blind to the fact that Tah and Phenom were out there. When the Lumina first pulled up, the two dudes climbed out and walked up on Vee asking for the dope stamped "Made In China".

When she served them, they went back to the car and returned with AK-47s, letting bullets soar in their direction. Phenom, on point as always, and caught the whole thing before they caught them completely off guard. Now one of them was laid out in the middle of the street with a bullet in his neck and two in his back.

Phenom and Tah stood in the middle of the street shooting at the fleeing Lumina, trying their best to hit the driver before he could get away. Phantom already had the Tahoe in drive with his foot on the brake ready to peel out. He knew they needed to make a quick getaway.

"Noooooooo!" Doug screamed, sitting on the ground as she cradled Vee in her arms. Vee's blood was soaking her clothes.

"Somebody call a fuck'n ambulance!" Jerm yelled, standing over Tabi who was on the porch, grabbing at her left shoulder.

Tah took a good look at the scene and tightened his grip on his 9-millimeter, turning towards the nigga laid out in his own pool of blood in the street. Phenom had run over to the Tahoe and climbed in thinking that's where Tah was going. Instead, he walked over to the shooter and stood over him and stared at him for two seconds, then asked, "Who sent you?"

"Yo, come on, nigga!" Phenom yelled from the backseat of the Tahoe.

"Nigga," Tah continued, ignoring Phenom as he contined to stare at the shooter. "Who the fuck sent you?"

"Vanessa!" Doug cried out, rocking Vee's lifeless body in her arms, tears running endlessly down her cheeks. "Pleasssee, God! Noooooo, take meeee!"

"That's so fucked up," somebody standing off to the side commented as onlookers watched the aftermath.

"Hang in there, Tabitha. Help is on the way. Just keep breathing," Jerm told Tabi, now down on his knees holding her right hand.

Tah had never killed anybody before but at that moment, he forgot all about that. As he leaned forward and pressed the barrel of the gun to the still breathing shooter's head, he said, "Fuck you and whoever sent you!"

Boc! Boc!

CHAPTER 17
Monday
September 29, 2014
In Trenton

"You just take it easy, ma. A bitch gon' take care of everything," Raye said, hugging his mother as they stood on her porch.

"I miss him so much," she replied, tears falling from her cheeks onto Raye's shoulder.

"I know, I know," he said, fighting back his own tears, while trying to be strong for his mother. He silently cursed out Bino for killing Todd. "You go on in the house. I gotta make a run."

"Okay, be safe, Raye. I love you, baby."

"I love you, too."

Raye tried to hide his tears from his mother, but she didn't have to see them to know that he was hurting just as much as she was if not more. Raye and Todd were extremely close. Still holding Raye close, she felt his heart beating through his chest, so she started patting him on his back to comfort him.

As a mother, she hated to see her only son like this because losing your brother was something that would always be hard to get over. Raye did have sister, but he was so much closer to his brother. Once Raye's mother released him from her grip, she took a step back and watched her baby walk away in pieces.

Raye may have been 41 years old, but he would always be her baby. He had been sitting around all week thinking about what to do to get back at Bino. He then walked down his mother's porch, heading to Leo's house. He wanted them how they could bring the beef to Bino's doorstep.

Raye couldn't understand how his brother allowed Bino to catch him slipping like that when he thought that they had the upper hand. Him allowing Bino to catch him off balance like that had cost him a lot. When the police got to the stash house, they found money, guns, and drugs, letting them know that it was personal and not a robbery. The case was wide open. Reading those details in the newspaper told Raye that noone else could've done but Bino. The beef had been nothing but personal after Todd and his boys killed Glee.

As Raye's mother turned back around to see her baby off, she noticed three masked men running towards him. She was so scared that she couldn't even muster up the words to tell him to look out. Raye had his head down thinking about how much pain Todd had gone through when he was killed, he never noticed Bino, Dez, and Rah running up on him with their guns drawn. Bino was within three feet was his mother finally had the strength to scream out to her son, but it was just too late.

"Raye, baby, look out!"

"Huh?" Raye gasped, lifting his head to see Bino nearly within inches of him.

Doom! Doom! Doom!

"Raye!" screamed his mother, dropping to her knees as Raye's whole left side of his face was blown off.

"Oh my God!" Raye's mother's neighbor screeched as she was forced to watch her second son being murdered before her.

Raye's body didn't get a chance to hit the ground because Dez walked up spraying bullets out of his AR-15. The bullets hit him all up in his upper torso causing his body to dance lifelessly. Dez smiled brightly watching Raye's body violently jerk from left to right.

The people looking through their windows were in complete disbelief watching evil in the flesh. Rah aimed his AK-47 at Raye's mother as she stood back up. He pulled the trigger sending countless bullets her way hitting her in her legs, and one in her chest before she collapsed.

Chunks of brick and wood fell on top of her as the bullets tore into her house as she laid on the ground praying silently as she felt the heat and pain from the bullets. Raye's mother laid there with blood pouring out of her mouth, trying to crawl down the porch in attempt to get to her baby, while Bino, Rah, and Dez stood over Raye ruthlessly emptying their guns into her body.

Bino was the first to turn around and run back to the dark green Ford Explorer where Young was housed in in the driver's seat. It was time to make their exit. Rah and Dez came up right behind him as he jumped into the backseat of the Explorer. They all knew their window of opportunity was closing quickly the longer they were at the scene of the crime.

"Young, let's go, nigga!" Bino barked once Rah and Dez were in the SUV.

* * *

7:31 p.m. In Newark

"Where are you?" Liz asked from their house phone, lying across the foot of their bed with the phone pressed against her ear.

"I'm out. You know that already," Tah replied, looking out of the window, thinking about Vee and Tabi as Phantom drove down Watson Avenue.

"Yeah, and look what happened the last time you told me you were out and about, why don't you just come home?"

"Liz, I just left the house like a half hour ago. I'm just now getting to the hood."

"Tahiem, why can't you just give it a break for a while?"

"Can we have this conversation when I get home later. I need to focus while I'm out here in the field."

"Whatever, bye!"

"Tell Liz I said chill out. You're in good hands," Phenom said, looking in the rearview mirror at Tah.

"She hung up," Tah told him, sitting his phone next to him on the seat. "Still no word on who did that shit to Vee and Tabi?"

"Nah, the news hasn't even released the name of the nigga that you killed."

Tah closed his eyes at the sound of those words, remembering the expression on the shooter's face just before he shot him. Tah opened his eyes, and said, "We need police in the pocket for shit like this 'cause we got a faceless enemy out there that knows exactly what we look like."

"How much?" Phantom asked, breaking his silence.

"How much what?" Tah questioned as Phantom made a left onto Elizabeth Avenue.

"How much are you prepared to pay to get police in the pocket, 'cause I know some people."

"Man, I don't know. I never done no shit like this!" Tah snapped, looking out of the window as he tried to figure out what he had gotten himself into.

Phenom enjoyed a good laugh at Tah's expense, then said, "Don't worry about it. I'ma get top of things and see what's what, but it might just cost you a nice little penny."

"Like how much?" Tah asked, thinking about the nice little stash that he now had.

"I don't know yet, but I'm gon' find out. Just be ready to pay 'cause it's gon' be costly."

"Damn!"

"Damn, what?"

"I'm already paying you, Tahiry, Doc, Tabi, the workers at the lab, and Phantom. And that's not including what I'm dishing out at home!" he replied, shaking his head weakly.

"Don't forget the Chadwick Girlz," Phenom laughed, adding to Tah's frustrations. "And the lawyers!"

"I'm glad you find this shit funny, mu'fucka."

"Aye, you wanted to be the boss, so you gotta suck that shit up. Ain't no sense in crying about it now," he told Tah as they neared West Peddie Street. "We're going to need to pay off more than one cop cause we got a lot of shit to move."

"A'ight, twenty grand is the max," Tah said, realizing he would be paying for Vee's funeral and Tabi's hospital bills.

"I'll make a phone call and set a meeting so you can meet with my cousin," Phantom said, knowing that his cousin could use the money.

"Cousin?" Phenom and Tah gasped in unison.

"Yeah, she works behind the desk in the precinct on 17th Avenue, but I'm sure she can point me in the right direction for a small fee."

"A'ight, bet! Set it up for tonight!" Phenom ordered.

"Where do you want her to meet us at?" Phantom asked, holding his phone in his left hand, driving through West Bigelow Street. "I can have her now."

"Nah, I'm not meeting nobody and from now on, my name Reggie," Tah informed him, thinking about how real things were getting by the day. "Nobody is to mention the name Tah ever again whether I'm around or not, understood?"

"Understood," Phantom answered.

"Phenom?"

"Do I get to change my name, too?" Phenom laughed, trying to get a smile out of Tah.

"Bruh, I'm serious as hell. I got a lot to fuck'n lose on this shit. I need you to be on board with me."

"I got you, I got your back, Reggie."

CHAPTER 18
Wednesday
December 25, 2014
7:15 a.m. In Roselle

"Mmmmmmm, shit!" Tah moaned as he grabbed a handful of the sheets, his toes curling. His eyes were tightly closed as he hungrily bit down on his bottom lip. "Fuck, got damn, L—Li—Liz!"

Liz had five of Tah's nine inches in her mouth, twirling her tongue around the head, while plunging and sucking it which was drove Tah above and beyord. Her mouth was unusually warm this morning with more spit than the day before. Her head jerked up and down on Tah's dick as she cuffed his nut sack and gently massaged them with her fingers. The whole time that Liz was pleasing him, she kept thinking about the red 2009 Lotus Exige parked outside in their driveway, it was causing her pussy to get drippingly wet.

Just the thought made Liz pop Tah's dick out of her mouth, spit on it, wrap her right hand around it, and stroke slowly. She moved down the length of his dick with her tongue circling his nuts before savagely sucking them into her mouth.

Sucking in a gargling fashion letting Tah's nuts dance on the back of her throat, Liz looked up at him with the meanest set of bedroom eyes. It was a no brainer that Tah lost his composure as his body forcefully jerked as Liz tightened her hand around his dick, enjoying every minute of it just as much as Tah.

The moment that Liz his mouth fell open numbly and his eyes rolled into the back of his head, she knew he was about to cum. So, she released his nuts and quickly gobbled down on his dick, stuffing all of him into her mouth.

"Aagggghhhhhhhhh!!" Tah exhaled, his ass cheeks clenching as Liz sucked his cum up out of him, swallowing it all with appreciation.

Liz twisted and turned her head as if she was sucking a lollipop, her eyes glued on Tah with the biggest smile on her face. She took three long hard slurps before dramatically releasing his dick from her mouth still stroking it, while stroking him. "Who dick is this?"

"Shit!" Tah said, laughing as he tucked his arms behind his head, looking down at Liz. "It's all yours. Ain't no argument there."

"And don't you ever forget it when you're out there with them thirsty ass hoes at the strip club!" Liz said, climbing on top of him as she purposely placed her warm, dripping wet pussy against his dick so he could see how wet she was.

"You got that, Mrs. Muhammad. Your head game is off the charts. With my eyes closed, I thought I was in the pussy for a minute."

"Nah, bae. For you, it's always wet. A bitch never ever had to use lip gloss!"

Liz kissed Tah on his chest before jumping up, leaving him lying there with the biggest smile on his face. She knew she'd put it down on him this morning. Tah had gotten in at four o'clock morning after he and Phenom were out in New York at Club Love. They were enjoying the money that felt like it came in by the second.

Liz was still in the bed when Tah came home so she had no idea that her gift had been in the driveway, Tah had Tahiry drop it off just hours earlier knowing that Liz wasn't going anywhere because he had the Tahoe. Even though he didn't celebrate Christmas he wasn't going to take it away from them, however, Liz knew that it was hard for Tah to go out and spend his money for such a holiday after explaining it to them just how Christmas had come about.

Tah knew Liz would be mad that he stayed out all night without answering his phone. So it was the perfect set up when she heard her garage door opening, quickly rushing downstairs to meet him at the door. However, when she reached the door, Tah wasn't there.

When Liz looked out of the door, she saw him standing next to the Lotus Exige with a huge smile upon his face. Tears instantly fell from Liz's eyes as she covered her mouth with her hands. She took off running towards him, still in her boy shorts and training bra.

Tahiry had told Tah that Liz told said she would love to have a Lotus, so he went behind her back and bought her one last week. He gave Tahiry the money to go out and buy it for her.

She allowed Tah to get in the shower so he could offer Fajr, his morning prayer, then she fucked the shit out of him for hours giving it her all.

Liz walked into their bathroom in their room and jumped into the shower. She knew it was only a matter of time before the girls woke up. Tah had quickly fallen asleep from the lack of it since he'd been running the streets like crazy lately. After Phenom and Phantom found two uniformed cops to add to the payroll, Tah opened up shop down on Camden Street in between 15th Avenue and 14th Avenue in the middle of the block.

He'd put Lissa, Chela, and Mona over there and they were slowly building the block up. Since there were other dudes over there, Tah and Phenom sat out there watching the girls' backs. Tah still had a lot of work left and he had to get rid of it so that he could get out of the game, little did he know, the game didn't just let go that easily.

* * *
Two Hours Later in Lafayette, New Jersey

"What seems to be the problem, Soo?"

"There's no problem. The lil' niggas picked up and moved so we don't—"

"That sounds like a fuck'n problem to me!" Jahad barked angrily through the phone, pacing back and forth inside his cell. "Now, let me tell you what's even worse. It's been two got damn months and you haven't found my shit!"

"I promise you that I'm on top of things out here. Just give me a few weeks and I'll have a smile on your face in no time," Soo replied, sitting there in his white $3,000 Gucci leather recliner.

"The only thing that you're on top of is that little hoodrat bitch you keep going down to Atlantic City to see, taking this bitch to Miami and shit instead of finding my shit!"

"That was just a little business trip that I had to—" Soo tried to get out before Jahad cut him off.

"Save it! Fuck a few weeks! You have until New Years day to have this thing under control or I'm gon' have you in a state of shock which is gon' bring grief to your entire fuck'n family!"

"Listen, you don't even have t—"

"No, you listen!" he snapped into the phone as if he wasn't in prison. "As Allah is my witness and my name is Mujid Jahad Muhammad Junior, if you don't have answers for me on the first, you're a dead man!"

Soo looked at his iPhone 3S in complete shock. Jahad never talked to him in that manner since they'd been dealing with one another, and honestly, he wasn't feeling it, but he had to deal for a while longer. He leaned forward and picked up his Cuban cigar that sat inside of his Crystal ashtray. He slowly nodded his head, acknowledging that what he had planned was the right move.

For the time being, he realized he had to come down off of his high horse. It was time for Soo to get back in the game and get his hands dirty. Soo was no stranger to putting in work and the streets were about to find out just how dirty he could get.

He took a pull of his cigar and then lifted his glass of $7,000 Remy Martin Louis XIII Baccarat. He took a healthy gulp, then picked up his phone again and dialed Pont's number. He swallowed the fine Cognac which was a French Brandy made in a small town in France named Cognac. Yeah, it's the same liquor as a cheap bottle of E&J.

"Rasool, to what do I owe this call on Christmas morning?" Pont asked, without properly greeting Soo.

"Do we still have eyes on the sister and brother?" Soo asked, twirling the cigar in between his middle and index fingers.

"Yup."

"Good, kill them mu'fuckas!"

"Huh?"

"Yeah, send them a little gift from me to him."

"Which body part?" Pont questioned, being completely caught off guard by Soo's sudden change in gangsterism.

"Neither. Kill them and put the word out that I'm not hard to find."

"Oh, I got it since we can't find him. Make him come to us."

"Exactly."

Duquie Wilson

CHAPTER 19
Meanwhile in Roselle

Bad boy ain't no good
Good boys ain't no fun
Lord knows that I should
Run off with the right one
Me and Mr. Wrong get along so good
Though he breaks my heart so bad

Liz stood in her kitchen listening to Mary j. Blige's *Mr. Wrong* featuring Drake. She was cooking her family a healthy Christmas breakfast with a huge smile on her face. Mya and Malani were in the living room surrounded by endless wrapping paper and toys.

Tah gave Liz and Tahiry both two thousand dollars to go out and get his babies everything that they could ever want. They were excitedly playing with everything they'd received. This was without a doubt the best Christmas that they had ever had.

Even though Tah hadn't taken Christmas from his family, he made sure to let his kids know that daddy bought them the gifts, and not some fat white guy named Santa Clause. Mya and Malani knew that Tah and Liz gave them this Christmas and nobody else could take that away from them.

They had an 8-foot tall white Christmas tree with red, black, and green lights around it, and a black angel at the top with an afro. Liz bought the girls fifteen black Barbie dolls a piece with the Barbie Dream House and car, an Easy Bake Oven, fake makeup kits, their own flat screen plasma TVs, bikes, coloring books and crayons, a PlayStation 2, Wii, XBox 360, two PSP's, and a shit load of clothes.

She had bought Travis a XBox 360 of his own and a copy of every video game that WalMart, Gamestop, and K-Mart had in stock. Because Travis didn't celebrate Christmas, Liz and Tah gave him his video game days ago. Tah took no part in buying or wrapping the gifts for the girls.

Liz was cutting up some green, orange, and yellow peppers along with onions and fresh mushrooms. She was cooking French toast, turkey bacon, beef sausage, scrambled eggs California style, and grits. Tah loved his eggs with the peppers, onions, mushrooms, and a pinch of garlic powder in them.

Liz had received her first gift at four this morning, but she hadn't received all of her gifts just yet. As Liz was mixing the vegetables with the eggs, the doorbell rang grabbing her attention. Travis was locked in his room playing his game with his surround sound on, so he couldn't hear the bell.

Tah was in bed asleep and the girls definitely couldn't answer the door, so Liz had to stop what she was doing and answer it herself. Liz wiped her hands on the kitchen rag and turned on her heels to go answer the door, smiling at the girls in the living room on her way.

"Hey!" Tahiry screamed, after Liz opened the door. She quickly embraced Liz in a loving hug, smelling the bacon seeping out of the house. "Merry Christmas, bitch!"

"Merry Christmas," Liz replied, with a huge smile on her face, spotting Doc down at Tahiry's car taking gifts out of the trunk.

"Where are my babies?"

"Tahi, keep it down. Your brother is still sleep."

"I know his Muslim ass is not still in that damn bed when his daughters are down here enjoying their Christmas!" Tahiry shot back, walking into the house in the best of spirits.

"Doc, do you need help?" Liz asked, standing in the doorway now feeling how cold it really was outside.

"I'm just taking them outta the trunk. Travis and Tahiem better get their asses out here and bring these shits inside!" Doc returned, looking up at Liz.

Liz smiled while shaking her head at Doc who was a sweetheart but had no problem cursing your ass out. She knew how to handle nearly any and every situation that came her way. Doc stood outside in a pair of black True Religion jeans, a black and red North Face snorkel, and a black New Era 59 Fifty Chicago Bulls fitted with a red bull on the front.

The bull had white horns with red tips, and on her feet were a pair of black Nike Air Jordan 16s with red and white accents. Since Doc had been transporting drugs for Tah, she was doing fairly well for herself. She now had forty pairs of True Religion jeans and nineteen pair of Jordans. She had her own studio apartment that was nicely furnished with expensive things, and the only one that knew where Doc lived was Tah.

* * *

An Hour Later in Newark

"You mean to tell me that that good for nothing ass nigga ain't even get you shit for Christmas?" Nurse Trisha asked, looking at her co-worker as if she had lost her mind.

"Uh huh. He said that he was Muslim and didn't celebrate holidays," Nurse Sheila replied, refusing to look up and lock eyes with the dark skinned girl.

"Yeah, fuck'n right. You just cooked his faggot ass pork chops last week for dinner."

"I know and when I said something about that, he got mad and stormed out of the house. I haven't heard from him since."

"And your ass better leave it just like that. If I was you, I'd change the fuck'n locks on the doors and wait for his ass to come home tryna use his keys!"

"Yeah, you right, 'cause he pull this shit every time a holiday comes up."

"He can only do to you what you allow him to do."

As the two nurses were heavy in conversation about deadbeat men they never noticed, the short woman walked past them in a black Chanel trench pea coat and right into China's room. Pont was sitting outside waiting for her to call him and to let him know the job was done. She was heavily debt and was on the verge of losing everything.

Pont came to her and told her that he'd give her $50,000 to kill someone for him. She felt it would be a piece of cake seeing as how it wouldn't be her first murder. But when he told her the person was in the hospital, she wasn't so sure about it anymore.

Then the thought of her seven kids out on the street flashed before her eyes and it was a no brainer. Pont had given her a silencer-equipped glock 9-millimeter and the floor and room that China was in. She didn't like what she was about to do, but she had to think about her kids who were now at home smiling because mommy had made things happen.

China was in her room lying in the same bed that she'd been in for the past few months. As the woman inched closer, China she moved her right index finger. The woman was taken aback as Pont told her that China was in a coma. People that were in comas didn't move their fingers the way she just did.

China had been lying there for a few minutes relaxing, while trying to move her limbs after finally waking up from her coma. She had been in the bed so long that her joints were stiff and achy.

The woman walked up on her and raised her gun, aiming it at China's face. She opened her eyes in disbelief, staring down the barrel of yet another gun after being in a coma for months because of a gunshot wound.

Looking down at China who was giving her a pair of pleading eyes, the woman wrapped her fingers around the trigger and said, "I'm so sorry."

* * *

Up the Hill On 13th Avenue

"Greg, run to the store and get some more milk," Stacie said, just now realizing that she was out of it.

"Really, yo?" Phenom shot back. He was sitting on the green leather couch he'd just bought watching the *Tournament* on Stacie's 60-inch flat screen plasma.

"Yeah, really!"

"A'ight."

"Don't say it like that 'cause I'm in hear cooking your ugly ass breakfast!" Stacie snapped, slamming the spatula down on the counter.

"I said, a'ight! Don't piss me off!" Phenom barked, pausing his movie before grabbing Stacie's keys off the living room table and proceeding towards the front door.

"Whatever, just hurry up!"

"Stacie, you know what, yo?"

"What?" Stacie barked, walking to the kitchen doorway and sticking head out so she could see him.

"Nothing, yo," he defeatedly replied, snatching the door open. "You just looking for a reason to be mad."

"I don't need to look for a reason 'cause just being in love with your stupid ass is more than enough!"

"Yeah, a'ight. I love you, too."

Phenom laughed as he stepped outside in his black Polo sweat suit, rushing towards Stacie's red Dodge Stealth that was parked across the street from her apartment. She'd been begging him to move her to another apartment or in with her.

The area was a dangerous thanks to the Bloods, but Phenom declined moving in. He didn't want her to move because GK told his homies to look out for Stacie. He felt his woman was safe where she was. He didn't know every big homie under other sects, so he was keeping her put.

Stacie saw how Tah moved Liz out to Roselle completely away from the hood they all grew up in. She wanted her man to do the same. Phenom was making $10,000 a month, but still refused to move Stacie. He was saving every penny he made so he could get his own thing rolling, but she didn't want to hear nor understand that.

After Phenom had climbed into the Stealth, Stacie came to door. "Bae, I need eggs and cheese, too."

"What else, Stacie?" he asked, sticking the key into the ignition.

"That's it, smart ass!"

"I'm just saying. I don't want you hurting yourself trying to call me to say you forgot this and that."

"Whatever. Just hurry up, please," she replied, as Phenom was pulling out of the parking space as a black Pacifica was coming towards him from 11th Street.

"Oh, shit! She has manners!" he yelled out of the window as the Pacifica sped up to block him in.

Sccccuuuurrrr!

"What the fuck!" Phenom gasped, pulling out his .45 caliber as the Pacifica nearly rammed the front of the Stealth.

"Oh my God!" Stacie mumbled nervously as three men stepped out of the Pacifica in black army fatigues with AR-15s in their hands.

Bok! Bok!

Tat, tat, tat, tat, tat, tat tat, tat, tat, tat, tat, tat, tat, tat tat!

"Oh my God! noooooooooooo!!!" Stacie screamed, feeling her heart completely shatter within her chest, watching her man get gunned down.

Phenom tried to shoot his way out of the situation he found himself in, but the gunman he had shot in the chest didn't so much as flinch as he returned fire with his AR-15. The three gunmen stood there in the middle of the street, emptying 50 round clips into the Stealth. They took no chances with Phenom after hearing about how he got down. The attack took only a few seconds, but to Phenom and Stacie, it felt like a lifetime.

Once their guns were empty, they calmly climbed back into the Pacifica and peeled off, leaving one hell of a scene for Newark police. The Stealth slowly rolled across the street crashing into a Toyota Camry that sat directly front of Stacie's apartment. Stacie was on the floor in her doorway continuously calling Phenom's name through endless tears. She could barely see as her eyes being filled with tears.

Duquie Wilson

CHAPTER 25
Minutes Later in Roselle

"It's about time you got your ass up. You can't be sleeping all day today. It's Christmas!" Tahiry said as Tah walked into the living room.

"Shut up. Where's Liz?"

"She's in the bathroom," Doc answered, sitting on the floor with Malani and Mya playing on their Wii.

"Good morning, ladies," Tah greeted, waving to Mya and Malani.

"Good morning, daddy!" they yelled in unison, never taking their eyes off of thee video game.

"Tahi, did you have enough to get everything?" he asked, hearing his cell phone going off upstairs.

"Yeah, and your godmother said you had better bring your ass over."

"What did she cook?"

"Ham, greens, roast beef, baked chicken, mac and cheese, cream of corn, yams, turkey stuffing, and potato salad."

"Got damn! Who is mommy expecting to come over? Barack and Michelle?" Tah laughed, very impressed with what he heard.

"Nah, she wants us all to come over there for dinner. If you ask me, I think she's getting lonely," Tahiry replied as Liz's cell phone began to ring, too.

"Shit, I'm there!" Doc said, thinking about all of the food.

"I'm going to brush my teeth. Tell Liz to wash her hands and make me a plate," Tah said, turning around as Travis stood there with Tah's phone in his hands.

Seeing the look on Travis' face, both Tahiry and Tah asked, "What's wrong?"

"Greg just got shot up outside of Stacie's house. She's on her way to the hospital now," Travis informed, tears now running from his young eyes.

"Oh my God!" Doc gasped, dropping the controller.

"Fuck!" Tah sighed, dropping his head shamefully. "Text her and tell her that I'm on my way."

"I'm coming with you," Doc said, getting up as the house phone began to ring.

Tah ran upstairs to get dressed leaving Tahiry down there speechless. They wouldn't be anything he could possibly say right now that would bring understanding of this whole situation right now. They hadn't even had time to get over the death of Vee, especially since he wasn't even buried yet, and now they had to deal this shit!

You had Tabi, who was at home dealing with depression over seeing her friend gunned down in front of her. Then she was fucked up over being shot herself. All of the Chadwick Girlz were loved the money they all were making.

But Tahiry was starting to wonder if it was all worth it. She asked herself who wanted money if they couldn't be happy spending it. She thought about the conversation she and Liz had the night Tah got into the chase with the Volvo S60. It all came back so clearly.

"I hope he ain't do nothing that will put us in danger," Liz said, sitting in that very same living room.

"Nah, Tah's too smart for that," Tahiry replied.

"I pray you're right because this money combined with the money he was throwing around, is really starting to scare me. I can't lose him like I did Ro,." Liz expressed just before he called her.

Now Tahiry was really asking herself if it was all worth it and where she sat in the whole equation, she knew she was in deeper than anybody else knew. Tah came back downstairs as the house phone continued to ring

He and Doc rushed out of the house with high hopes that Phenom was okay. Once Tah and Doc were out of the house, Tahiry realized the house phone was ringing. She walked over to the coffee table and grabbed the phone. "Hello?"

"Good morning, this Nurse Greene from University Hospital, I'm calling to speak to Elizabeth Kimbrough in regards to her sister, Nicole Kimbrough."

"Hi, Ms. Greene. This is Nicole's other sister, Tahiry," she replied as Liz came walking into the living room with a pregnancy test in her right hand.

"I'm pregnant!" Liz announced, while Tahiry was listening to Nurse Greene trying to understand what she was saying. Her facial expression told a story in itself. Liz stopped smiling and asked, "What's wrong? Who are you on the phone talking to?"

Tahiry dropped the phone as tears poured down her cheeks after what she'd just heard. Her world was slowly crashing down on her. She looked up at Liz after breaking down to her knees and said, "China is dead!"

To Be Continued...
The Streets are Calling 2
Coming Soon

Submission Guideline

Submit the first three chapters of your completed manuscript to ldpsubmissions@gmail.com, subject line: Your book's title. The manuscript must be in a .doc file and sent as an attachment. Document should be in Times New Roman, double spaced and in size 12 font. Also, provide your synopsis and full contact information. If sending multiple submissions, they must each be in a separate email.

Have a story but no way to send it electronically? You can still submit to LDP/Ca$h Presents. Send in the first three chapters, written or typed, of your completed manuscript to:

LDP: Submissions Dept
Po Box 870494
Mesquite, Tx 75187

DO NOT send original manuscript. Must be a duplicate.

Provide your synopsis and a cover letter containing your full contact information.

Thanks for considering LDP and Ca$h Presents.

<u>Coming Soon from Lock Down Publications/Ca$h Presents</u>

BOW DOWN TO MY GANGSTA

By **Ca$h**

TORN BETWEEN TWO

By **Coffee**

BLOOD STAINS OF A SHOTTA **III**

By **Jamaica**

STEADY MOBBIN **III**

By **Marcellus Allen**

BLOOD OF A BOSS **V**

By **Askari**

LOYAL TO THE GAME **IV**

LIFE OF SIN

By **T.J. & Jelissa**

A DOPEBOY'S PRAYER **II**

By **Eddie "Wolf" Lee**

IF LOVING YOU IS WRONG… **III**

LOVE ME EVEN WHEN IT HURTS **II**

By **Jelissa**

TRUE SAVAGE **VI**

By **Chris Green**

BLAST FOR ME **III**

A BRONX TALE

By **Ghost**

ADDICTIED TO THE DRAMA **III**

By **Jamila Mathis**

Duquie Wilson

LIPSTICK KILLAH **III**

CRIME OF PASSION **II**

By **Mimi**

WHAT BAD BITCHES DO **III**

KILL ZONE **II**

By **Aryanna**

THE COST OF LOYALTY **II**

By **Kweli**

SHE FELL IN LOVE WITH A REAL ONE **II**

By **Tamara Butler**

LOVE SHOULDN'T HURT **III**

RENEGADE BOYS **II**

By **Meesha**

CORRUPTED BY A GANGSTA **III**

By **Destiny Skai**

A GANGSTER'S CODE **III**

By **J-Blunt**

KING OF NEW YORK III

By **T.J. Edwards**

CUM FOR ME **IV**

By **Ca$h & Company**

GORILLAS IN THE BAY

De'Kari

THE STREETS ARE CALLING

Duquie Wilson

KINGPIN KILLAZ II

Hood Rich

STEADY MOBBIN' **III**

Marcellus Allen

SINS OF A HUSTLER

ASAD

HER MAN, MINE'S TOO **II**

Nicole Goosby

GORILLAZ IN THE BAY **II**

DE'KARI

TRIGGADALE II

Elijah R. Freeman

Available Now

RESTRAINING ORDER **I & II**

By **CA$H & Coffee**

LOVE KNOWS NO BOUNDARIES **I II & III**

By **Coffee**

RAISED AS A GOON I, II, III & IV

BRED BY THE SLUMS I, II, III

BLAST FOR ME I & II

ROTTEN TO THE CORE I III

By **Ghost**

LAY IT DOWN **I & II**

LAST OF A DYING BREED

BLOOD STAINS OF A SHOTTA I & II

By **Jamaica**

LOYAL TO THE GAME

Duquie Wilson

LOYAL TO THE GAME II
LOYAL TO THE GAME III
By **TJ & Jelissa**
BLOODY COMMAS I & II
SKI MASK CARTEL I II & III
KING OF NEW YORK I II
By **T.J. Edwards**
IF LOVING HIM IS WRONG…I & II
LOVE ME EVEN WHEN IT HURTS
By **Jelissa**
WHEN THE STREETS CLAP BACK I & II III
By **Jibril Williams**
A DISTINGUISHED THUG STOLE MY HEART I II & III
LOVE SHOULDN'T HURT I II
RENEGADE BOYS
By **Meesha**
A GANGSTER'S CODE I & II
By J-Blunt
PUSH IT TO THE LIMIT
By **Bre' Hayes**
BLOOD OF A BOSS **I, II, III & IV**
By **Askari**
THE STREETS BLEED MURDER **I, II & III**
THE HEART OF A GANGSTA I II& III
By **Jerry Jackson**
CUM FOR ME
CUM FOR ME 2

222

CUM FOR ME 3

An **LDP Erotica Collaboration**

BRIDE OF A HUSTLA **I II & II**

THE FETTI GIRLS **I, II& III**

CORRUPTED BY A GANGSTA I & II

By **Destiny Skai**

WHEN A GOOD GIRL GOES BAD

By **Adrienne**

A GANGSTER'S REVENGE **I II III & IV**

THE BOSS MAN'S DAUGHTERS

THE BOSS MAN'S DAUGHTERS II

THE BOSSMAN'S DAUGHTERS III

THE BOSSMAN'S DAUGHTERS IV

THE BOSS MAN'S DAUGHTERS **V**

A SAVAGE LOVE **I & II**

BAE BELONGS TO ME

A HUSTLER'S DECEIT I, II

WHAT BAD BITCHES DO I, II

By **Aryanna**

A KINGPIN'S AMBITON

A KINGPIN'S AMBITION **II**

I MURDER FOR THE DOUGH

By **Ambitious**

TRUE SAVAGE

TRUE SAVAGE II

TRUE SAVAGE **III**

TRUE SAVAGE **IV**

TRUE SAVAGE **V**

By **Chris Green**

A DOPEBOY'S PRAYER

By **Eddie "Wolf" Lee**

THE KING CARTEL **I, II & III**

By **Frank Gresham**

THESE NIGGAS AIN'T LOYAL **I, II & III**

By **Nikki Tee**

GANGSTA SHYT **I II &III**

By **CATO**

THE ULTIMATE BETRAYAL

By **Phoenix**

BOSS'N UP **I , II & III**

By **Royal Nicole**

I LOVE YOU TO DEATH

By Destiny J

I RIDE FOR MY HITTA

I STILL RIDE FOR MY HITTA

By **Misty Holt**

LOVE & CHASIN' PAPER

By **Qay Crockett**

TO DIE IN VAIN

By **ASAD**

BROOKLYN HUSTLAZ

By **Boogsy Morina**

BROOKLYN ON LOCK I & II

By **Sonovia**

GANGSTA CITY

By **Teddy Duke**

A DRUG KING AND HIS DIAMOND I & II III

A DOPEMAN'S RICHES

HER MAN, MINE'S TOO

By Nicole Goosby

TRAPHOUSE KING **I II & III**

KINGPIN KILLAZ

By **Hood Rich**

LIPSTICK KILLAH **I, II**

CRIME OF PASSION

By **Mimi**

STEADY MOBBN' **I, II**

By **Marcellus Allen**

WHO SHOT YA **I, II**

Renta

GORILLAZ IN THE BAY

DE'KARI

TRIGGADALE

Elijah R. Freeman

GOD BLESS THE TRAPPERS I, II, III

THESE SCANDALOUS STREETS I, II, III

FEAR MY GANGSTA I, II

THESE STREETS DON'T LOVE NOBODY I, II

Tranay Adams

<u>BOOKS BY LDP'S CEO, CA$H</u>

<u>TRUST IN NO MAN</u>

<u>TRUST IN NO MAN 2</u>

<u>TRUST IN NO MAN 3</u>

<u>BONDED BY BLOOD</u>

<u>SHORTY GOT A THUG</u>

<u>THUGS CRY</u>

<u>THUGS CRY 2</u>

<u>THUGS CRY 3</u>

<u>TRUST NO BITCH</u>

<u>TRUST NO BITCH 2</u>

<u>TRUST NO BITCH 3</u>

<u>TIL MY CASKET DROPS</u>

<u>RESTRAINING ORDER</u>

<u>RESTRAINING ORDER 2</u>

<u>IN LOVE WITH A CONVICT</u>

<u>Coming Soon</u>

BONDED BY BLOOD 2

BOW DOWN TO MY GANGSTA

ABOUT THE AUTHOR

Duquie Wilson was born on November 2, 1985 in Newark, New Jersey where he spent majority of his life learning the tricks of the trade of how to survive and adapt in nearly any and every situation. He has been writing since 2006 and is a self-published author of several novels such novels as *B.P.M. - From Pups To Men, Thoughtless Survival, 07065 - Prison City, Undistinguished Life Span, Anticipate: What You Eat Don't Make Me Shit* and *Brim La Familia: The Dopeboy Story.*

Duquie Wilson has also spent some of his childhood in Oxford, North Carolina as well as Rahway, New Jersey. He is the proud father of Janayah, Christopher, Jakaii, Bryonna, Marlyn, Elijah, and Alyssa. He currently resides in his hometown of Newark, New Jersey, and is working on his next novel.